JOURNEY THROUGH DARKNESS

Peter Cordwell

MINERVA PRESS

ATLANTA LONDON SYDNEY

JOURNEY THROUGH DARKNESS
Copyright © Peter Cordwell 1999

ISBN 1 75410 639 X

First Published 1999 by
MINERVA PRESS
315–317 Regent Street
London W1R 7YB

Printed in Great Britain for Minerva Press

JOURNEY THROUGH DARKNESS

To Joshua
I hope you get as much pleasure from reading this as I did in writing it – all the characters are fictional but it is based on historical fact.

It is set in approximately 2800 BC.

About the Author

Peter Cordwell retired from a career in local authority in 1991, at the age of forty-one, mainly on health grounds, as he suffers from Friedreich's Ataxia which is a progressive neurological condition. Although he is in a wheelchair he is an inveterate traveller and is a fairly frequent visitor to the Middle East and parts of Africa. He is fascinated by the Cradle of Civilisation and is an amateur historian of ancient Middle Eastern history, among his other interests, which include a lot of work for disability-orientated organisations, organising holidays and he is a trustee for his own charity. His talent for writing stories was only recently recognised while writing a story for his nephews, from where *Journey Through Darkness* originated.

Preface

O dearly beloved, come with me across the vast areas of time to a place far, far to the south and the east, to the furthest shores of the inland sea, to a time when the world was young and beautiful and mankind was in his infancy.

We are now in a place where the great river meets the sea. The place will later be called Alexandria, and the river, which is still a great river, was then called the Isis or the river Nile, by which name it is still called today. We are in a land called Egypt, which is ruled by Pharaohs who were kings of mortal men and became gods when they were throned.

These Pharaohs were minor gods amongst the many gods who were placed over men. The principal god was called Aamon Ra who shared the rule of men with his brother Seth. However, Aamon Ra loved the daylight and the sunshine and all things that grew under the sun, indeed he was the sun god and is often pictured as a bright orange disc, but Aamon Ra's brother, Seth, did not like the sunshine and grew to hate all the beautiful things that his brother created. Seth was a creature of the night and he created the demons and wild things that come out in the night as well as the evil things in world that kill and cause suffering.

Chapter One

Our story begins with a prince who was the son of a king. The king was now a Pharaoh, as he had taken over the throne when his father died and therefore he was no longer a mortal man, but was a god-king or Pharaoh, the leader of his people. It was his job to look after his people, to lead their army into battle, to ask the other gods to make the great river overflow every year to water the land and enrich the soil, so that the plants would grow and the people would have plenty of food to eat. This Egypt was a great land because of the great river which came far from the south, from beyond the bounds of Egypt and from nowhere that anyone had been or at least from where no one had ever returned – for indeed many had tried, but all had failed.

Our little prince was called Nementhoteptha Pthah Akron (which was a bit of a mouthful, particularly for someone so young, so we shall call him by the name that he preferred to be called, which was just Nem) and he lived in his palace, or at least one of his palaces, that was situated on the great river.

Nem often wondered why his father who had once played with him and taught him many things and used to laugh and tell him wonderful stories by night before he went to sleep no longer did. Now he never came to see him any more, but would send one of the courtiers to request the young prince to attend his father's presence. Although his father still looked like his father had looked, he was somehow different; Nem was told that this was because his father was now a Pharaoh and therefore a god.

Nem was taught many things by his teachers, but they could never make Nem clearly understand how his father had become a god. Nem often asked his teachers, 'Does that mean he will never die, like the other gods?' but he was told that his father would die but then would relive his life as a god in the second world where he would never die. Nem was also told that this would happen to him as well, because when his father died, Nem would inherit the throne and therefore become a god, just like his father. Although this worried Nem, because he did not really understand about the main gods, minor gods, and god-kings, he used to try to forget all those big problems because his life was very enjoyable. Amongst all his teachers, there was one teacher who was his favourite. This teacher was called Chithra and he seemed to know more all than the other teachers put together.

The young prince was very pleased when on his tenth birthday he was told that as well as being taught his normal lessons he would also be instructed how to fight, not just man-to-man fighting, but also how to lead an army and win battles. He was very excited when he was told that all his teaching would now be under the care of Chithra. Nem seemed to spend every day with Chithra whom he loved dearly as although he was very wise, he was also a lot younger than many of the teachers and was very kind to Nem and always had a ready smile and often told him funny stories.

The time that Nem liked best was when Chithra and he would take a few days and walk away into the hills and live like the desert nomads, camping out under the stars and eating what food they could either pick or kill, like nuts and berries and wild rabbits and even snakes and lizards. It was very often on these outings that Chithra taught Nem a great deal about fighting because although Chithra was not a great fighter himself because, as he told Nem, the gods had not made him very strong, he was very athletic and very fast, in movement as well as thought. He often told Nem that to be a great warrior a man had to act quickly and also had to *think* quickly so that he didn't fall into a trap that was waiting for him. On many of their outings they would take a small boat out on to the great river where Chithra used to teach the young prince how to catch the fish in the river and also how to swim in the river but to be respectful of the great beasts within it like the crocodile and the most dangerous of them all, the hippopotamus, or river horse as it was sometimes called. The strange thing about the hippopotamus was although it never ate flesh, as did the crocodile, it could never be trusted and could very easily snap a man in half in its huge mouth with its great ivory tusks.

On one of their outings, Nem was rather careless and he did not notice the presence of a hippo, (which is what they called them for short), and this hippo surfaced beneath Nem's boat and he fell in the water landing on the hippo's back. The hippo was just as surprised as Nem but he hated being touched so he twisted his great neck and snapped his mighty jaws at Nem. The hippo threw Nem off his back causing Nem to strike his head against a rock which not only made his head bleed, but almost knocked him out as well. Although Nem managed to swim to the bank he was very slow in his movements and had it not been for a well-aimed spear from Chithra, the heir to the throne of Egypt would have ended up as a crocodile's next meal. It was then that Nem realised that not only was Chithra a great teacher but was indeed a wonderful friend who looked after Nem like a father would have.

Nem did not understand why Chithra made him wear a very heavy copper and stone bracelet when he was practising his sword fighting, and also why he made Nem wear heavy boots made of a wood and leather when they marched or walked long distances. The copper and stone bracelets made his sword arm heavy and slow, as indeed did the heavy boots so that he always seemed to be lagging behind Chithra. Then one day, it must have been when Nem was about fourteen years old, he and Chithra were walking along, deep in discussion, talking about how the stars and the sky changed their position according to the time of year, when all of a sudden they turned a bend in the road and came face to face with one of the huge lions that often came up from the South. Although the lion was as surprised as they were, lions are not afraid of men and it prepared to spring at them. Chithra reacted instantly, turned and bounded away calling Nem to follow him as quickly as he could. Nem's reactions were almost as quick and he was very soon chasing after Chithra, and because he wasn't wearing his big boots his long legs quickly overtook Chithra and they were well away from the lion before it could attack them. Nem then realised why Chithra made him wear the boots and indeed the heavy bracelets – they had made his legs and arms grow very strong and he could now run very fast. Even at the age of fourteen he was as tall as Chithra and his long gangling arms and legs were developing very strong muscles so that he could run for long distances without getting tired and also fight for a long time before his sword arm became weary.

It was shortly after the encounter with the lion that Nem asked Chithra about how and why he would become a Pharaoh or god-king when his father died, and indeed why did his father have to die because he was still a big strong man, a mighty warrior and was loved by all his people. Chithra told Nem that even though his father was a great man, even the greatest could be killed in battle by a single arrow that was well placed. So, no one knew the time or the place and even Chithra would be very sad when Nem's father died because he was a good and wise Pharaoh and looked after his people and this very Egypt which was their home. Chithra then went on to explain about the work that he was overseeing about the Pharaoh's tomb, where Nem's father would be buried and then go into the other world to become an immortal god. He also told Nem of what would happen to his father's body, about how the embalmers would remove parts of his body and place them in special stone jars and the rest of the body would be sewn up again and covered in deep oils and wrapped in bandages to preserve it for the next life. Seeing how interested in all these things the young prince was, he continued telling him of the journey that his father would have to make in the underworld. He explained to Nem that as the underworld was below ground it was ruled by Seth and how his father's mummification was necessary so that the pharaoh would be able to perform all the tasks necessary for him to become a god. Chithra then explained to Nem that all these things were told of in *The Book of the Dead* which was cut into many stone tablets that were kept in a special room in the temple that was part of the palace. Indeed Nem had heard of this very ancient book, which his teachers had spoken of only in whispers.

Chapter Two

Nem recalled his long conversation with Chithra, and he promised himself that he would learn more about the whole business of what would happen when his father died. He did not have long to wait, because only a week later he was summoned to see his father, to see the plans that his father was making for his own burial. Though Nem was rather frightened by the whole business, he dutifully went with the guard who had summoned him and they went right down to the forbidden areas of the dungeon of the palace where Nem knew he could see the stone tablets on which *The Book of the Dead* was kept.

His father was surprisingly friendly, and put his arm around his son's shoulders in an unusual show of affection. He then told Nem that a lot of the treasures that were in the palace would be stored in his funeral chamber, so that he could use them in his next life. However, he would still leave a lot of things behind that Nem would then become responsible for, as when he died Prince Nem would then ascend to the throne of Egypt, change his name, and become god-king, the next Pharaoh. His father asked his son's opinion, and simply said that this was the way it had always been since the beginning. They then went into a small room next to where *The Book of the Dead* was kept and his father showed him the intricate plans for the underground maze of tunnels that would eventually lead to the burial chamber. His father said that one of the biggest problems that all the Pharaohs faced was how to protect their treasures so that grave robbers did not steal them before they could be used in their second life. Nem was very surprised that anyone should dare try to enter a burial chamber and steal things that were buried there.

His father sighed and said, 'Yes, my son, there are many such evil men in this world, for only a few days ago we found that your grandfather's tomb had been broken into, and most of the treasure had been stolen.'

Nem was silent for a long time while he contemplated all these things and then his father surprised him even more when he said, 'Follow me and I will show you what happened.'

Feeling that he was in a dream, Nem followed his father out of the palace and on to one of the great papyrus galleys that sailed up and down the great river. As they stepped on to the galley, the guard sprang to attention and as soon as the Pharaoh and Prince Nem were seated the mighty galley left the shore and went up river for about two and a half hours until they came to a great statue of a cat with a man's face. This Nem knew as the Sphinx and it was said to guard the Valley of the Kings. Here they left the galley and went on foot, accompanied by three of the royal guard. After a ten minute walk across the rocky desert they came to a small cliff where a pile of rocks had seemingly been pushed down from above. On closer inspection it appeared that the rocks had been cut from a doorway that opened into the cliff above them where they stood.

Pharaoh motioned to the captain of the guard. The man's name was Thylux and he was one of the strongest and mightiest warriors in the army. Thylux stood with his back to the cliff and as one of the other guards ran at him, he grabbed the man's foot and literally threw him up the rock face so that he landed on the new doorway. Within seconds a rope ladder had been secured and they all went up the ladder to stand by the dark opening in the cliff. The

guards, and even Thylux, seemed frightened and it was
Pharaoh who led the way into the doorway with Nem
following close behind and the guards reluctantly following
behind them. Pharaoh grasped a torch that one of the
guards lit for him using his tinder-box. Pharaoh then led
the small band holding the torch above their heads. Long
shadows were cast by the flickering torchlight which barely
lit the tall passage as it opened out before them. Pharaoh led
the small company turning first right, then taking the
second left and a further right to where the passage split,
one level going uphill to the left and another going down
on the right side. Here Pharaoh stopped and read the
hieroglyphics cut into the wall and paused as if searching
deep into his memory. He then chose the right-hand
passage which wound down and down until he finally
stopped and pointed to a gap in the floor just in front of
him. He led his men carefully around this hole in the floor
and as Nem passed he could see down into the depths of
the pit which was full of spikes upon which a corpse was

impaled. It had obviously been there for quite a while as it had started to decay. Pharaoh led them on, seeming to remember the passage but at each turning he marked a symbol on the wall with a piece of charcoal. After many minutes and many turns and many passing traps that opened the floor beneath them, the passage suddenly opened into a wide space from where many things had recently been moved. This was evident because there were marks on the floor showing where things had been dragged away. At the far end of the room was the large stone tomb, which Nem knew was called a sarcophagus, in which the body of the old Pharaoh had been laid. Pharaoh led the way towards the sarcophagus, which, when Pharaoh held his torch above it, was seen to be empty. They all gasped, because they knew that the mummified body of the Pharaoh was laid beneath a solid gold death-mask, which carried a curse of death to the man who stole it.

'Our bloodline must be avenged,' murmured the Pharaoh, 'if our Egypt is to remain safe. And this must be done within the next five years, for it is written that if a Pharaoh is moved before he can enter the other world his lineage will last only as long as those left remaining alive.'

In a trembling whisper he then said to Nem, 'I am the third in this line; this, Nem, makes you the fourth. Therefore, to become Pharaoh after me you must avenge my being unable to enter the other world.'

After a long silence, they then made their way back following the markings of charcoal on the wall, but what had once been a timid band led by a strong figure became a terrified band with Nem supporting his father who seemed to have aged by twenty years. They came out of the newly opened cavern into the fading glow of the evening, and somehow made their way back to the galley that was waiting on the great river.

As soon as they were aboard and the galley had started back downriver towards the palace, Chithra appeared and seemed to take charge of the proceedings. Giving Nem's father one of his strong potions to drink, he said, 'Pharaoh is tired and must now sleep.'

Chapter Three

Nem was deeply troubled by the events of the previous day, particularly about the fact that he had to avenge his grand-father's death, which meant finding the missing body of the long-dead Pharaoh and restoring it to where some of the treasures had been stolen.

He went in search of Chithra and found him still look-ing after his father who now seemed a lot better but still looked older than he had before, mainly because his hair had turned grey. When Chithra saw him coming, he very quickly realised that Prince Nem had some very important questions to ask him because he looked worried. Leaving the Pharaoh in the care of the other doctors, he took Nem outside on to the palace roof and asked him what was troubling him. Nem told him about what his father had said and that Nem, although he hadn't said he would do it, felt his father had automatically accepted that it was his son's responsibility to avenge his grandfather's theft.

Chithra considered all that Nem had said for a long time, looking deep into Prince Nem's eyes, and he then said, 'Yes, Nem, it is your responsibility, but do not worry because you have five years before you must do this thing and we must use every day of those five years to prepare you for this very difficult task, because it will mean you going on a long and dark journey.'

Nem shuddered at the thought of this long journey, because although he was fast reaching manhood he was very aware, but he tried never to show, that he was still afraid of the dark. Even though he realised that his fear was not very rational, he still couldn't help it. He was about to tell this to Chithra and he opened his mouth to speak, but Chithra silenced him with a finger.

'Don't worry about your fear of the dark because it is better to be afraid of something that you do not understand, and we have these five years to try to shed that fear and replace it with sensible caution.'

Chithra then left Nem because he had some urgent business in the palace. Nem at first felt annoyed that his old teacher could read his thoughts so well and thought that perhaps he showed his fear of the dark. However, the more he thought about it, the more he realised that it was probably only Chithra who fully understood him and he was then filled with greater love for his teacher.

Nem then wandered off to the gymnasium in order to do his daily sword practice. He still used the weights around his wrists (the copper and stone bracelets) whilst he was practising so that when he would actually fight in battle he would be very quick and not easily tire from wielding the heavy bronze sword that he used. He went through the standard twelve moves that all fighters are taught with a few extra ones that he had devised with Chithra's help. This he did time after time, gradually getting faster and faster, until an hour had passed and he had worked up a good sweat. He then took off his stone and copper weights and put them down beside his royal gold bracelets. He then looked up as the noise of new captives being herded into the gymnasium caught his attention.

He picked up his sword belt and followed the newcomers to a part of the gymnasium that had only recently been extended. The gymnasium, although it was part of the palace, was really an outbuilding and it joined on to the soldiers' barracks and was well away from all the stone and marble staircases that were everywhere else in the palace.

The floor through the gymnasium was the ordinary earth floor like a parade ground. Nem quickly realised that the newcomers to the gymnasium were a band of Hittite warriors who had been captured at the battle of Quartar. This was a battle that was totally unexpected as Quartar was just to the north-east of Egypt where the Red Sea ends and just before the desert lands of Sinai. What had happened was that a large force of the Egyptian army was returning home from the campaign against one of the Canaanite armies, which they had soundly beaten, when they came across a band of soldiers from the Hittite army that had been scouting far south of their normal areas. As the Egyptian force was far larger than the Hittite, the Hittite general had quickly surrendered, realising that his men would stand little chance.

Now, the normal procedure when there is such a battle and one side surrenders is that the surrendering soldiers are offered a choice – to fight for the army that they surrendered to, provided that every single man swears a personal oath to the new king or in the Egyptian situation the Pharaoh, or be killed. Now some of the Hittite warriors were very tough battle-hardened soldiers who would not normally surrender at all, but would rather fight to the death. However, as this band had been ordered to surrender and had been constantly used in one campaign after another for the Hittite king, who was building up his empire to the north, they had all almost welcomed the opportunity to fight for the Egyptian army, which was far more disciplined and did not wear out the soldiers, allowing them to have plenty of leave and generally paying them good wages. Therefore these warriors had quickly taken the opportunity to fight for the Egyptians and accordingly gave their allegiance to the Pharaoh.

The guard captain who was in charge of them was the very same Thylux who had accompanied Nem with his father, the Pharaoh, when they had entered the grave-robbed tomb. Now it was time to see how good the surrendering warriors were. Thylux paired the warriors off and put them through their paces at individual combat, each pair fighting in a ring marked with stones.

Finding a convenient seat, Nem watched a pair of the warriors to see how good their swordsmanship was. The two warriors that he was watching were both young men, possibly a bit older than Nem, but they looked both very fierce and strong men, particularly the nearest one, who, although he was not very tall, or not as tall as Nem, was very broad across the shoulders and deep-chested and stood on strong, powerful legs and was very quick with his sword and shield. As Nem was watching them he saw a red sand scorpion that had come into the ring and was poised to strike at the nearest opponent, who had not noticed it. Reacting without thinking, Nem picked up a stone and hurled it at the scorpion – he was deadly accurate and the rock splattered the scorpion before it could strike. Unfortunately the rock bounced on and hit the soldier on the back of his calf – fortunately it did no damage but it was quite painful. The soldier yelled in pain and looked around for the person who had thrown the stone.

As he saw Nem, he called out, 'You coward, rather than throw stones why not come and fight me like a man.' This challenge was shouted out across the gymnasium and everyone looked round. As Nem was not wearing his gold bracelets that depicted his position as a prince it was understandable that the strange soldier did not realise who he was challenging.

Although Nem did not want to really fight this strange tough-looking soldier, he always felt that most of the opponents who had fought him in training sessions had always allowed him to win as they did not want to offend him, but rather wanted to be a friend of Prince Nem because it would be to their advantage to have a royal friend. So before he realised exactly what he was doing he stood up, buckled on his sword belt and took his place in the stone ring facing the Hittite warrior. He accepted the shield that the other soldier gave him and drew his own sword which was an answer to the challenge.

A hushed silence had fallen over the gymnasium as they watched what happened. No man dared to intervene for fear of Prince Nem's annoyance and, secretly, they all wanted to see just how good he really was, because he had never been bested in battle. Captain Thylux stood with his hand ready on his sword to intervene in case Prince Nem looked like getting injured, because Thylux, like most of the guard captains, liked the young prince as he was not arrogant or big-headed, like many proud young men can become.

The two young men eyed each other coldly and each man weighed up the looks of the other. The Hittite soldier realised that this young opponent was obviously powerfully built, perhaps not with the raw strength that he possessed, but he saw that his opponent was half a head taller than he was and judging his strong arms and legs, realised that he had a battle on his hands.

With a sudden cry the Hittite warrior sprang across the stone circle with a powerful downward slicing swing of his sword arm. All of a sudden this slashing movement was transferred into a killing thrust aimed at Nem's neck. Rather than raising his shield, Nem used this to cover the vital organs of his body and easily parried the thrust taking the full force on his sword and diverting the blade so that he came underneath the Hittite's sword arm. The Hittite warrior realised that he had almost misjudged his opponent and with lightning speed regained his balance and came at Nem again with a killing thrust aimed at his belly. Once again Nem parried his blow quite easily but realised that the Hittite warrior was very, very quick. Once again the Hittite warrior attacked and once again Nem deflected the stroke that was aimed at his right side. Very soon both men were sweating heavily because of the hot sun bouncing off the walls of the gymnasium. It always seemed to be the Hittite who was attacking, and Nem never seemed to be able to get an attacking movement going. There was a gasp from the onlookers as Nem seemed to stumble and the Hittite poised ready for a cutting and killing stroke. But Nem had only appeared to have stumbled and with amazing cat-like agility twisted himself around, catching the Hittite's sword arm with his shield and moving behind him, suddenly had his own sword at the Hittite's exposed throat.

'Yield!' he called, 'Or your blood will stain the ground.'

The Hittite's sword fell to the floor with a clang and the Hittite fell on to one knee before his victor.

'I yield,' he cried, 'My name is Buryl, and you have beaten me in a fair fight. I subject myself to your mercy as you are a better swordsman than I. To whom do I surrender?'

'My name is Prince Nementhoteptha Pthah Akron,' he said, 'and I am the son of the very Pharaoh to whom you swore your allegiance to protect. But I would rather be your friend than your enemy as you are a stout and brave fighter, so please call me Nem. But I am no coward. It is true I threw a stone,' he said as he flicked over the stone with his sword to show the crushed scorpion beneath it. 'Indeed I am glad that my father has such soldiers as yourself in his army.'

'Apologies, my lord,' said Buryl, 'I had not realised the stone was not meant for me. Indeed you have my friendship and I extend my oath to protect your father, to protect you as well, as it is an honour to serve such a good swordsman.'

Unnoticed by the crowd, who were all watching the contest with baited breath, Chithra had entered the gymnasium and had watched the fight and the new friendship being formed, and smiled warmly as he glanced across to Thylux, who sighed with relief as he removed his hand from his sword hilt.

Chapter Four

As the two young men became friends they often tried to get away from the palace and their allotted duties. It didn't seem to matter to either Nem or Buryl that Nem was a prince, so to a large extent Nem did what he wanted to – once his lessons and armoury practice were finished for the day. Buryl was just an ordinary soldier, and in fact a stranger to the land of Egypt. However, because he had no family, once his duties were over he was entirely free. Their greatest pastime was when they were out among the reed beds on the great river, where they spent a long time spear fishing. This was an art that Buryl taught Nem because although the fish had to be near to the surface of the water to be seen, the spear had to be aimed a little forward from the object because it seemed to bend as it entered the water.

On one such occasion the young men were aboard Nem's papyrus boat and were fishing alongside one of the grand reed beds trying to spear the great river perch that lay in wait of smaller fish. They were a great delicacy but were very difficult to spear due to their ability to move so quickly. Nem saw a sudden movement and hurled his spear at where he thought the perch's head should have been, but as the spear flew through the air towards the spot a horrible snake-like head leaped at him through the water and with one mighty snap of its jaws, it cut the spear into two pieces.

'By the gods,' cried Nem, 'that was a mighty perch.'

'No, Nem, called Buryl, 'that was no perch but one of the mighty freshwater eels. It must have been washed down from the mountains when the river flooded last month.'

These great freshwater eels were normally only found in the mountains where the river flowed very fast and made deep pools. Buryl came from such a mountainous area far to the north where another mighty river, called the Euphrates, started its long journey down to the sea. Both young men wanted to try and catch the eel and as Nem reached for his second spear – they were both standing each at one end of the papyrus boat – they realised that they would not have long to wait. The great eel, as thick as a man's thigh and all of three cubits long, was snaking its way towards their boat.

As it hit the boat right in the middle, its jaws clamped, cutting out a huge hole in the papyrus, but at that very instant both spears flew at the mighty head as it came to the surface. Both spears were thrown with deadly accuracy and with sufficient strength to not only pierce the flesh but penetrate right to the massive backbone of the eel and with two such spears hitting it on the back of its head together the eel's body curved in one mighty spasm as it died.

Both young men were thrown into the river by the impact, but both witnessed the death of the great eel as they were flung into the river. They quickly swam to the dead eel and each grabbed it by their spears and dragged it to the bank of the river and pulled ashore their catch. All of this was done before any of the giant Nile crocodiles, which were sunning themselves on the sandbanks of the river, could smell the blood of the eel and slip into the river and swim towards the commotion.

The two fishermen were delighted with their catch and it was as much as the two of them could do to carry it back to the palace, where they presented it to the astonished cook. Prince Nem demanded that it should form the centrepiece of that night's banquet.

There were forty people gathered around Pharaoh's dinner table that night where there was plenty for all of them; the freshwater eel is a great delicacy. Also, because it is normally only caught in the mountains this means it is not usually so fresh when it is served. Obviously there was great praise given to the young men who had speared such an eel and the story was told and retold on many occasions and both Nem and Buryl were revered as great spear fisherman.

A few days later when the two young soldiers were in the gymnasium, Chithra suddenly appeared and called them over to inspect gifts that he had for them. Each was a beautifully weighted ebony spear with one of the eel's teeth forming the point that was honed to needle sharpness. Each tooth was bound securely on to the split ebony with copper wire that was twisted in strong, decorative shapes – like the original eel. As both young men stared at the beautiful weapons, Chithra said, 'These weapons I have had made especially for you, and I hope that they will be of use when you take the long journey through darkness.'

Until then Nem had forgotten about the long journey that he had agreed to make, but was very glad that Chithra had already chosen him a partner to journey with him when the time came.

Chapter Five

So the days wore on with more and more training and the occasional fishing trip. They still went out into the hills to spend nights under the stars, the only difference being that with Chithra still in charge Nem had Buryl to accompany him. On these outings they always ate extremely well as both young men were excellent hunters as well as being good spear fishermen. They were also fortunate there, because amongst his other skills, Chithra was an excellent cook.

On one such outing about a year after the young men had speared the great eel, they were sitting around the campfire finishing the remains of an excellent meal of fruit roasted with guinea fowl, which Nem and Burl had shot with their bows and arrows.

Without looking up from his dinner Chithra said, 'About the journey that you must make, I have to tell you that it will be fairly soon when you start. Although there are theoretically two years before you must go, the longer you leave it the harder the trail will be to pick up. One of the problems is that this very Egypt is being challenged by the empire to the north.'

He pointed at Buryl to indicate that it was the Hittite empire to the north where Buryl had come from.

Nem was about to interrupt, when Chithra silenced him with a finger and continued with his story of what was happening in the world. He told them that there was a kingdom a long way away where the Euphrates enters the sea and that this new kingdom, called Babylon, was willing to trade with Egypt and that the trade would be of benefit to both empires. He went on to tell them wonderful tales of far off places like Persia and India where lots of very unusual woods, beautiful jewels, wonderful silks, as well as gold and silver, came from. He said that Babylon lay at the gate to the route to India and Persia and they were willing to trade many of the articles for a lot of the ivory that Egypt brought from the tribes and wonderful cotton and linen cloths as well as the many jewels that were found in the mountains far to the south. He said that this trade was just the beginning and could greatly increase the wealth of Egypt and that Egypt had nothing to fear from Babylon.

However, he then went on to tell both young men that the first large caravans (the name given to a large convoy of traders carrying their goods on the backs of camels) had been attacked and robbed. At first they thought that this was by a band of warlike nomads, but when the next caravan had also been attacked there had been a small battalion of Egyptian army guarding the traders, and it was then realised that the attackers were fully trained soldiers of the Hittite empire. It was realised that the Hittite empire was very keen to get its hands on the goods from both Egypt and from Babylon, but that the Hittite empire did not have much to trade with.

Therefore, there was probably going to be a war between the Hittites and the Egyptians. Once again Chithra had to silence both young men who seemed eager for the opportunity of battle. Now Chithra agreed very quickly with the young men that on its own the Hittite army was no match for the Egyptian army but he then told the young men about the alliance between the Hittite empire and the Phoenicians (who were often called the sea people). He went on to explain about the Phoenician ships which were made from wood, and that they outmatched any of the enormous papyrus galleys that the Egyptians had.

He further explained that the wooden galleys could hold a lot more men as they had hollow hulls and were not just a mat of reeds; they were also a lot more manoeuvrable in the sea and a lot faster. He then explained that this alliance between the Phoenicians and the Hittites meant that the Hittite army could be moved by sea on the Phoenician galleys, and they could therefore attack the Egyptians almost where they wanted to and that any possible battle at sea would bring certain destruction to most of the Egyptian ships.

As Chithra paused before continuing, Nem asked, 'But why haven't we built wooden galleys, if they are so much better?'

Chithra replied, 'One of our very scarce items is trees, not just palm trees, but the right type of trees that yield wood to make the galleys, and there is a lot of skill in shipbuilding that we do not possess. We have only recently become aware that we have been slow to realise the advantage of these wooden galleys, both for military and merchant use.'

Here Buryl joined in the discussion.

'We have the advantage of knowing the Hittite tactics, as quite a few of the senior soldiers who were captured with me are now senior soldiers in our Egyptian army.'

Chithra acknowledged this to be correct, but went on to explain that fighting from ships (which he called naval battles) was entirely different from fighting on land. He said that one of the most feared weapons at sea was that of fire, because fire could destroy ships very quickly and rather than being able to shoot back at the enemy the sailors on the galley had to try and extinguish the fires. Additionally it was far easier to set fire to a reed boat than to a wooden boat, and then he reluctantly admitted that once again the

Phoenicians were far more advanced than the Egyptians because they used something that they called Greek fire, which consisted of pots of liquid that were flung from the catapults on the ships and which had a burning fuse and when the pot struck its target it would shatter and everything that the liquid touched would burn.

All of a sudden, Nem interrupted Chithra and said, 'All of this is jolly interesting and we must obviously attempt to catch up with the enemy. I suggest we must try to capture some of their ships and learn their secrets. But even so, what has this got to do with my journey?'

'You must realise,' continued Chithra, 'that a lot of people are well aware of the prophecy about the grave-robbed tomb of your grandfather, that unless his mummy is found and laid to rest with its rightful treasures, everyone will expect us to be beaten by the Hittites so that your line is ended.'

They were all silenced then for a long time, each man lost in his own thoughts.

Finally, Nem stood up and said, 'We must hang about no longer, for tomorrow morning we must go back and get ready to start our journey.'

'Yes,' Chithra said, 'I have already made a few plans. Firstly, a small wooden boat is at this very moment being made ready for you, designed by a deserting Phoenician sea captain.'

Very early in the morning, just as the sky to the East was beginning to show the first glow of morning light, the three men were already up and striking camp. Carrying their few belongings they started their hike back towards the palace and the guard camp. It was still early morning when they arrived back at the city where the palace was situated. It was bright by now but still fairly fresh as the sun had yet to warm the buildings and the air around and within them. This was the time of day that Nem liked the best and he often used this time of the day for a refreshing swim in the river before breakfast. There was no danger of crocodiles so early in the morning as being cold-blooded animals they had to allow the sunshine to warm them up before they could move around quickly. Also the hippos, although they were warm-blooded, tended not to be active first thing in the morning.

They made their way through the waking city to the palace, where the guard rose to meet them and said that Pharaoh was asking for all three of them to attend him. So they quickly made their way to Pharaoh's main chamber. When they entered, Pharaoh was deep in conversation with the guard captain, Thylux, but he broke off his conversation as they entered and went over to Nem to speak to him.

'I believe that Chithra has already told you that you have to make plans to start your journey, because I dare not lead our people into battle against the Hittite army or the Phoenician navy whilst our line is unavenged.'

He put his arm around his son's shoulders, noticing for perhaps the first time that his son was as tall as he was and although Nem was not as sturdy as his father, he was lithe and powerfully built with broad shoulders and long-muscled arms and legs that seemed to glow with inner strength in the morning sunlight.

He put his other arm on Buryl's shoulder as he led both young men back towards the main table where Chithra was deep in conversation with Thylux.

Then, almost casually Pharaoh said to Buryl, 'I release you from your oath to fight for me and my son, but hope you will go with him anyway because that is what friends are for.'

He continued speaking, but to the whole company this time, 'I am sending Thylux with you,' he said, 'as he has requested to go and was present when the robbery was discovered. He is also the best and mightiest warrior in the army and it is important that this quest is accomplished quickly before any of our people lose confidence in my leadership of the army.' Pharaoh continued, 'But your party can be no larger than three. Indeed, I would send you Chithra if I could, but I will need him as one of my chief counsellors.'

They all gathered around Chithra who was bending over a map that he had spread out on the table, secured with weights.

'This,' he said, 'shows the course of the great river, which you must follow up from the Valley of the Kings – where most of the treasures must have been taken by boat or raft upriver – and up past the second and newer kingdom of the upper Nile, up beyond the first cataract of the river, which passes the boundaries of our land.'

Chapter Six

Chithra said that just outside the palace there was the new boat that had been built for them and they needed to measure carefully how much extra room they had on the boat after they were on it with their war gear. This would tell them how much room they had for provisions on the journey.

It worked out that they had a lot more room than on a conventional raft, but it was still important to choose things that they could eat that were high in energy yet low in weight, and also things that they could not buy or kill on their journey. Here, Pharaoh interrupted and gave them a large bag of gold coins for the journey that they could use to exchange for food on their journey – as most of the tribes they would meet in the south, which they would pass through, already did a lot of trade with Egypt for things that were common in their land. Pharaoh interrupted Chithra again, and sternly told Nem that although he was officially in charge of the posse, because he was a prince, he should leave all the decisions about leadership to Thylux. They started to make a list of everything that they must carry. A surprising amount of cargo was for cooking and for the lighting of lamps, because they were not sure where they would be able to buy refills of oil for their stoves and torches.

It was the following morning, fairly early, when they all met down on the jetty outside the palace, where the new boat was moored on to the quay. It looked magnificent with the gently curving prow and stern posts and with the two oars either side which could be used when the wind was blowing in the wrong direction. Yet although the boat was big enough for the three of them it still looked remarkably fragile when compared to the enormous reed galleys. They were soon to learn how tough the little craft really was. The mast lifted out of its fixing point and so did the keel board which projected down beneath the boat, so that they could pick up the boat between the three of them – walking with it upside down on their heads. It was also capable of running through very shallow water, especially when the keel board was drawn up. They carried the minimum of weapons – each man had his shield and sword and two daggers. They all carried a small bow with a few arrows and also a spear. Nem and Buryl carried the new spears that Chithra had made for them with the long ebony shafts tipped with the mighty eel's teeth. But Thylux carried an even longer and heavier metal spear with a broad, bronze point, which could slice as well as kill with a thrust. They carried only one small double-bladed axe, that would be used for chopping wood – not for fighting. They carried only their war gear and one spare set of clothes and a single blanket each, because they were told the further south they went the hotter it became.

They all quickly stowed away the gear and paused briefly to say goodbye. To each one Pharaoh gave a small gift – to Thylux he gave a copy of his own seal that he wore around his neck, to signify that he was in charge of the band and Pharaoh's official envoy. To his son, Nem, he gave two new silver and gold bracelets to show that he was a prince among men and also a stone on a gold chain which he placed around his son's neck. He said the stone, which caught the light and glistened in every direction, was a great diamond which would light their way in dark places.

Then, in an embarrassed silence, he said to Buryl, 'I have thought a long time about what I should give to you, my son's greatest friend and sworn protector, I therefore have decided to give you one of Egypt's greatest treasures, one of the great rings of power that I wear. I give it to you to wear with honour and trust. It is this marvellous blue ring of lapis lazuli that is said to give its wearer long life and good fortune.'

Pharaoh then turned sharply on his heel and walked quickly away from the quayside and with one final hug to each man from Chithra and a few well chosen words of wisdom, he also turned and left. The three men boarded their boat with prince Nem taking the first oars and Buryl behind him with the second pair of oars and with Thylux standing proudly in the stern holding the tiller. Quickly they moved out to the centre of the great river and were soon well away from the city, which soon disappeared beyond the horizon.

They had rowed south for perhaps two hours, before a breeze sprang up coming from the north, so they could unfurl the large, triangular sails which hung from a sloping boom pole. They billowed out catching the wind which sped them southwards. Passing the Sphinx that guarded the entrance to the Valley of the Kings, they sped south down the great river, passing many towns and villages where people were busy in the fields preparing for the harvest. They then travelled past the town called Papay, which was where the large sheets of paper that were made from papyrus were made. Nem remembered this town from when he was a small boy and he had been with Chithra, who had taught him about how the sheets of paper were made from the cut and dried lengths of papyrus that had been flattened and stuck together with a special resin. This resin was extracted from lotus flowers seen often on the quiet stretches of the river. In the late afternoon they crossed the line marking where the new kingdom of the upper Nile started. Although this kingdom was inferior to the northern kingdom where the Pharaoh reigned, it had a lot of natural resources and was fast becoming more and more important. The breeze freshened into a strong wind and they were all surprised at how fast the small boat sped through the water. Whizzing along, keeping well out of the way of the hippopotamuses and the crocodiles that were wallowing in the shadows, they sped on southwards, until late on in the evening when they came to the great city of Luxor which is where the king of the southern kingdom reigned. Here they stopped for the night, sliding along to a vacant spot on the quayside just as it was getting dark.

They were met on the bank by a small party that had come down from the new king's palace by the river. Two courtiers came forward from the party and approached Thylux, recognising him as they came. They bowed in greeting and said that the new king had been forewarned of their arrival and had prepared dinner for them, with a message that he would be happy to give them a place to sleep for the night. Thylux thanked the courtiers and said that they would greatly welcome the chance to dine with the king and sleep in comfortable beds, as they were now entering uncharted waterways. They soon made the boat safe for the night, folded up the sail, checked that their belongings were safely secured and wore only their ceremonial daggers, as it was considered bad manners to attend a palace dinner in full war gear. They then made their way, surrounded by the party who had come down from the palace, back to the main hallway where they were welcomed most courteously. The king of the southern kingdom had been to the north to Nem's palace some five years previously. He smiled graciously and said how glad he was to see Prince Nem, and remarked upon how Prince Nem had grown into a fine young man. Nem remembered the king also as an ordinary man who was a lot shorter than his own father, but who held himself with a kingly bearing. He was therefore quite a lot smaller than Nem, who, when he looked around realised that, apart from Thylux, who was still a hand's span taller, he was bigger than all the king's own guards in this new palace.

The king introduced his own household starting with his daughter who was named Vavia, a dark-skinned, extremely beautiful, lively girl, with violet eyes which seemed to grow larger as they gazed up at Prince Nem in sheer wonder. Nem looked down in astonishment at the young princess who was only a year younger than him and he completely missed the other introductions that the king made about his own household.

Nem introduced Buryl as his lieutenant, but said that Thylux was captain of the party, so Thylux sat at the king's right hand, with Nem on his left, next to the Princess Vavia, who much to Nem's surprise and delight engaged him in intelligent and witty conversation and they soon found that they had much in common and were indeed very attracted to each other.

After they had dined on venison that had been hunted earlier that day, and had all eaten their fill and drunk a lot of the very pleasant wine that the king prepared for them, he dismissed many of his guests before he spoke to them about their reason for their journey. The king told them that there had been a rumour a few years previously about a large amount of treasure that had been taken upriver, but explained that his investigations as to how it came south or who was in charge of its carriage led him nowhere. But it was possible that the people from just above the town of Aswan, where the first cataract of the river was to be found, might know something of it. He told them that these people were called the Sudanese and their country was called Sudan. He then went on to say that they were on a dark and perilous quest, but he realised how important it was and therefore wished them all the help that the gods could give.

Thylux thanked the king for this information which, he said, would be most useful – and thanking the king once again for the excellent meal, he excused himself, Nem and Buryl, by explaining that they had to continue their journey early the next morning and that they had travelled a long way today and were very tired. They all slept a comfortable and peaceful night, but rose again just before light so that they could continue their journey as soon as the sun was up. Once again they rowed away from the palace in the light of the early morning and were so pleased to see the ripples on the water, stirred up by the breeze that again blew from the north, once again they unfolded the sail as their little boat sped them southwards.

Very soon they had left the city of Luxor well behind them and they then passed a small island where a new palace was being built. This was said to be a massive structure that could house Pharaoh and his household when they came south, as they often did in the wintertime. Leaving this little island behind, which was called the Island of the Elephant, although no one really knew why, they noticed that the river was flowing faster at this point than anywhere else that they had seen it and heard a roaring noise which was coming ahead of the boat. They therefore drew the boat into the side of the great river and decided once they had made it to shore to walk up river to see what was happening to make such a noise. After buckling on their swords and carrying their shields, because there were said to be wild tribes in this area near the border, they set off following the river. They soon saw that the noise came from the first cataract, where the river fell in great gushing spouts that scored a deep channel in the rock. It was indeed a very peculiar sight and quite a wonder for Nem, who had heard of it but had never seen it before. They decided that the best way would be to carry the boat around, because there was a good path and to try to haul the boat up the waterfall would be extremely difficult. But as they turned to go back to the boat Thylux spoke to both the young men.

'Don't look behind you, but there are at least two no-mads hiding in the hills, so we must be very wary when we bring the boat up, with one of us on guard, while the other two do the heavy work of carrying the boat.'

This they did, but of course it took a lot longer because the boat was very heavy for just two people to carry, so they had plenty of stops and changed places often. It was while Nem was on guard for the second time, that he saw a movement in the rocks up above him to the left. He called out to Thylux and Buryl to rest for a minute, which was only just in time because a heavy rock came bounding down the cliff from the rock face and smashed into the ground just in front of the boat. Buryl and Thylux quickly fastened their sword belts and Buryl grabbed his bow and threw Nem's bow to him and Thylux grabbed his large spear. As small rocks were thrown down at them there was a cry as one of their attackers was shot by Nem. As Nem was above the other two he could see three of the attackers waiting with a boulder to pounce, and he called a warning to Thylux. Thylux, however, had already moved himself to one side of the path as the attackers sprang out at them. The first attacker's head was cut from his shoulders in a mighty sweep of the long spear carried by Thylux – this was all too much for the attackers, who were only a small band of ruffians who had never fought such strong trained soldiers before, and they ran into the hills.

'I don't think we'll have anymore problems with them,' said Thylux, as he wiped off the fresh blood on his spear.

'You did well,' he said to Nem, pointing to the dead man lying on the path with an arrow in his leg. 'Your warning shout was very timely.' Nem knew, however, that Thylux hadn't really needed the warning. Thylux proved to be correct and they had no further problems as they brought the boat to just above the waterfall. Here they sat down and had some lunch, adding to the wheat cakes that they carried some dates that grew by the river.

Realising that they were now in this new country called Sudan they marked the area with a crude scoring on the rocks that said, 'You are now entering Egypt, the Land of Pharaoh.' They then relaunched their boat into the calm water above the falls and resumed their journey southwards.

Chapter Seven

Having satisfied their appetites, they reboarded their small craft and once again sailed on south in this new land. After a couple of hours the wind died down and they had to bring out the oars and row further south for an hour or so. It was difficult to realise that they were in a different country because the river looked very much the same, although perhaps less wide. There was still the occasional sandbank where crocodiles basked in the sunshine. They pulled into the bank near a few date palms as they had decided to make camp fairly early and scout around the area on foot. Thylux dismissed both the young men and said that he would set up camp, and told them to try to find something to eat and to scout round the area.

Nem and Buryl picked up their bows and arrows in the hope of shooting something for dinner. They scouted around on both sides of the river, which they swam across, but the whole area seemed deserted of wildlife although the ground was very heavily marked with the hooves of many animals who had recently crossed the river, but the tracks were a few days old and they seemed to have devastated the plants growing in the area. Then suddenly Buryl touched Nem on the shoulder and pointed up in the sky where there were vultures hovering on the wind.

Buryl said, 'See, the sun birds have seen something dying a few miles to the south-west.'

As this was on their side of the river they trotted along carrying only their bows and arrows and they soon found what the vultures were hovering over. It was one of the strange animals from the herd that had made the hoof prints, but it was a young animal that had gone lame and had not been able to keep up with the rest. They had no great problem in outrunning this strange animal, which had a big shaggy front, as it limped along on uncertain legs. They were almost doing the animal a favour in killing it quickly as it would have eventually fallen prey to the vultures as it gradually weakened. Putting a couple of arrows in its leg was no difficulty and the animal was not big enough to give them any great problems in carrying it back to Thylux. By that time Thylux had set up camp and had a small fire going beside the river. Thylux said that he had seen this animal on a previous journey into Sudan and said that they called the animal a wildebeest and it went in search of new pastures as it came from the south, where the dry season was almost at an end and the plains there had no grass on them. The meat was extremely tasty and there was plenty left over for breakfast and the next day, which they salted and stowed away in the boat before sleeping for the night, taking turns to keep watch – although nothing disturbed them all night long as they lay under a blaze of stars.

In the morning they reboarded the boat and rowed off after a quick breakfast of cold meat. Shortly afterwards the wind came up again blowing from the north so they were able to make good progress under sail. They kept going through lunchtime taking it in turns to steer whilst one rested and ate lunch, one kept watch in the bows and another steered the boat from the tiller at the back. By the afternoon they noticed the speed of the water was again increasing, but there were no high rocks or cliffs around them, so they just kept out of the very fast current where water was deep but not fast-flowing. Here they kept a close watch for hippos as they saw the telltale signs where they had wallowed in the muddy shallows and, sure enough, further on they came to a long bend in the river where some hippos were feeding on the papyrus that grew in the shallow water on the outside of the river bed. They thought it would be best to use the oars and move into the faster water rather than risk getting accidentally crushed by the beasts and were glad when the strength of the current died down and the wind once again sprang up and they could use the oars and unfurl the sail. They camped again by the river and spent another quiet night, before sailing on early the next morning.

As they sailed Nem pondered the fact that he had dreamed every night since he had met the beautiful dark princess about what would happen to her if his own kingdom should fall. Hardly realising that he had fallen in love with this beautiful young princess, he hoped with all his heart that his quest would be fruitful, meet with full success, and that he could then safely unite the two kingdoms by taking Princess Vavia to be his queen.

He quickly snapped back into reality as he realised that ahead of them the river split in two and between the river flowing from the south-east and the river flowing from the south-west, a town stood on the land between the two rivers. It was obvious that in order to decide which course to follow they needed to make a certain number of investigations, so they headed for the largest building in the strange town, which stood on the confluence of the two rivers. They moored on the quayside between two small fishing boats from the local town and as they made fast the ship a crowd of townsfolk gathered curiously around to observe the strangers, obviously such because of the way they dressed and because of their paler skin. Thylux and the two young men buckled on their full war gear before they left the small ship. A crowd of townsfolk gathered around them, keeping a few paces away, forming a large ring around the newcomers. Thylux held up his hand with an open palm in a gesture of peace and he spoke in the broad common tongue of southern Egypt which he hoped the Sudanese would understand.

He said, 'We come in peace. Would you be good enough to take us to your leader.'

A self-appointed spokesman called back in the same language, 'Friend, come with me and I will take you to the chieftain of our city which is called Khartoum.' Without even waiting for a response he continued, 'I gather from your dress that you come from Egypt in the north and that this is an important quest that you are on as you wear the seal of the Pharaoh around your neck.' The man's quick darting eyes looked them over very quickly and he said, 'I see that one of you is a prince, but he is not the leader of your party.' He continued, 'My name is Creallus and I am one of the main merchants of the city.'

Buryl said to Thylux and Prince Nem that he would remain on guard by the boat as the others would not need his assistance in speaking with the chieftain and it was far better for him not to come and to keep guard of their belongings. So Thylux, followed by Nem, went with Creallus into the strange city, which was full of narrow streets, and seemed to have been built in bits and pieces with no plan, which was totally unlike Egyptian towns. Creallus led them up through the winding streets and alleyways until they reached a small square which had a hall at one end where there were guards at the doors. However, these guards, although they were large by Sudanese standards, were half a head shorter than Nem and were therefore totally dwarfed by Thylux. They immediately stood aside and opened the door for the strangers, who were led in by Creallus who then made the introductions.

The Sudanese chieftain looked more like a Bedouin than a town-dweller and Nem felt that he seemed out of place in a stone building. The chieftain held up his hand in an open palm signal of peace and inquired as to the nature of the strangers' visit and asked them how he could be of assistance.

'We come on a quest,' stated Thylux, 'as one of our long-dead Pharaohs was stolen from his burial chamber along with his treasure.' He waited for his words to sink in then continued. 'We also believe that you may know the perpetrators of this crime against great Egypt who we represent.'

'Well, my friends,' smiled the chieftain, 'come and sit with me. Take your refreshment while I tell you a story.'

He clapped his hands for his servants to attend them. Thylux and Nem sat on the heavily embroidered cushions as they listened to the rambling tale that the chieftain told them. He told them that about two years ago, or perhaps longer, a band of Watutsi warriors from the south had passed through the town and were said to be carrying something that they had stolen from the north. He explained that the Sudanese people were merely merchants and tradesmen and did not fight battles and that Watutsi warriors were very tall and very fierce-looking. He looked at Nem and he said, 'They were of your height, my lord prince, but they were not built as strongly or powerfully as yourself and were certainly no match for your giant commander,' he nodded and turned to Thylux, who asked if they wanted to trade any of the treasures, whether they took them for a particular reason, where these Watutsis came from and what was their purpose.

'My lord,' said the chieftain, 'they often come from a kingdom a lot further to the south, and they trade with ivory tusks taken from huge beasts called elephants and with the pointed horn of the black rhinoceros, a terrifying beast whose running thunders the very earth. They also wear necklaces of teeth that they have taken from the great apes of the jungle.'

Nem thought for a while, and then asked, 'But they gave you no indication of what they wanted to use the old Pharaoh's body and his treasure for?'

The chieftain turned to Nem and said, 'No, lord prince, all they told us was that none of what they carried was to be traded.'

'So there was another purpose,' said Thylux.

'Yes,' said the chieftain, 'of that I am certain, but what they needed the items for is a mystery. But this I can tell you – they do have some very strange and unusual beliefs, particularly with regard to the ivory teeth from the elephants. There is a legend about the elephants' graveyard, which nobody has ever seen, but presumably it would contain many such teeth.'

After a moment's silence, Thylux asked, 'When did you last see these Watutsi warriors?'

'They have not been seen since, my lord,' said the chieftain, 'but we do know that they have promised to return with more ivory teeth and normally come around now or the next few weeks, certainly before the end of the dry season, because they have to journey back south before the rivers start to overflow with the coming of the rains.'

There was a long pause while everything that had been said was considered. The chieftain then clapped his hands and more refreshments were brought in and the conversation turned to more mundane matters, concerning trade and the fear of a new empire to the far north of great Egypt. After a while, Thylux and Nem felt that they would find nothing further of great interest. They thanked the chieftain for his help and said that his aid would be remembered when it came to any further trade between the two countries.

Then, after bowing politely to the chieftain, Thylux and Nem took their leave and returned to the quayside where they found Buryl cooking some fish which he had bought from the fisherman for their dinner.

Chapter Eight

They stayed in Khartoum for another two days, making further inquiries amongst all the traders and dealers about goods that came from the tribes to the south of Sudan. They discovered that the Watutsi tribe came up the right fork of the great river, either on primitive rafts or dugout canoes or sometimes, if the river was in full flood, by foot. Further enquiries led them to understand that they could travel upriver for three days before they encountered the next cataract. Then they discovered (or rather overheard people saying) that they had not been touched by any of the warlike raiders because of what they had done on entering Sudan. The news of their minor skirmish with the brigands while they were bringing their boat up the cataract had spread before their progress and nobody had dared to try to stop them. And indeed it was quite obvious that a lot of the common folk were suspicious of their ornate dress, their size and the deadly weapons that they always carried with them. Particularly, of course, Thylux, who seemed a real giant to these Sudanese people.

They were staying in a small tavern right beside the river, so that they could keep an eye on their boat and they had just made plans to leave the next day when they heard that a band of Watutsi warriors, with gifts to trade, had been sighted about two days' march from Khartoum. So they decided to stay where they were, and put the word out to all the traders that as soon as this warrior band was sighted they should be directed towards the tavern to speak to the men from Egypt. Whilst they were waiting for this band to show up, they made further enquiries about the Watutsi people, but learnt nothing more than the Sudanese chieftain had told them.

Later the next day, after an evening meal, whilst sitting in an alcove of the tavern, their conversation was interrupted by a messenger boy, who informed them that the Watutsi leader was on the way to the tavern. They had already agreed with the owner of the tavern to use a back room for their meeting, so they went into the back room and all three of them put on their war helmets, making them look even taller and more formidable than they already were.

A few minutes later there was a knock on the door and the innkeeper came in. Behind him was a tall slim black man dressed in a long flowing gown and his height looked even greater than it was as he had large strange feathers in his hair; these feathers were black, white, large and very curly and none of them knew, or dared even guess what strange bird they had come from. The very small innkeeper looked up at Thylux who had Nem standing at his right hand and Buryl at his left, all three looking taller in their helmets crested with eagle feathers.

He introduced the Watutsi chief who was standing behind him, 'This is Ingrit. He has come here to trade with our people, and he may be able to help you as he has some knowledge of what you are asking about.' After this brief introduction, the innkeeper looked relieved at having said his piece and beat a hasty retreat out of the room, ensuring that the door was carefully closed behind him.

Thylux, still standing in his helmet, said, 'Greetings, Lord Chief, we have waited to meet you and hope that you can be of assistance to us in a quest which we have undertaken.'

Ingrit remained standing, even though he was shown a chair on which to sit. He looked into Thylux's eyes sharply, raising his head only slightly as he stood nearly as tall as Thylux himself. He looked proud and was not intimidated by the three large men who stood before him. He simply said that he had come with fifty pairs of huge teeth taken from the great elephants that were to be found in vast herds to the south of Khartoum and also horns from the rhinoceros, curled and twisted horns from the kudu and teeth from the great black apes.

After a pause, Thylux said, 'I am sure that you will be able to trade these things in this city, but it is information that we seek and we can offer gold coins for information about a body that was taken from our country along with the treasure that was buried with it. This we believe,' he added with a grating voice, 'was taken by your people.'

'I know nothing of these things,' said Ingrit proudly and turning to go he said, 'Your gold does not interest me as I too can trade in gold that I bring from great Zimbabwe, to the south of our country.'

As he moved toward the door, Nem blocked his path and placed an arm on Ingrit's shoulder. Ingrit's eyes blinked when he saw Nem's gold and silver bracelets and there was real fear in his eyes when next he spoke.

'I know nothing of what you seek,' he told them.

Nem thrust him down on to a chair and Buryl drew his sword and held it at Ingrit's neck.

Thylux said, 'Your head will stand on the mast of our ship unless you answer these questions truthfully. Firstly, what do you know of a long-dead king whose grave was robbed by your people? Where is the treasure that was taken with the body?'

'I had nothing to do with the robbery,' wailed Ingrit as he fell on his knees pleading for mercy. 'All I know is that our gods need your gods to drive away the fierce warriors from the south!'

'You obviously know a great deal more than you have already told us,' said Thylux in a menacing voice as he sat on a chair with his face only a few inches away from Ingrit's.

'But it was not I who stole from you,' wailed Ingrit, 'and the men who did were ordered to do so by the black witch of Mutluc.'

'So you do admit that your people stole from great Egypt,' said Prince Nem.

'How have you come back to haunt us?' wailed Ingrit as he looked with horror at Prince Nem's bracelets. Thylux beckoned to Nem and Buryl as he stood by the door leaving the huddled Ingrit shivering with fear.

'He believes you are the long-dead Pharaoh, because of your prince's bracelets, as they have your grandfather's marking on them,' whispered Thylux to Nem, 'but I think he speaks the truth when he said that he did not steal himself.'

'But he knows who did,' said Buryl, 'of that there can be little doubt. He is absolutely terrified of Nem as he thinks he is the long-dead Pharaoh come back to life.'

'Yes,' said Thylux, 'but we must learn more of this story of their gods needing our gods to help them and about this black witch of Mutluc. I think we must use his fear of you, my prince,' he said to Nem, 'so you must now continue the questioning.'

They sent Buryl to bring in refreshments which Nem put on a table and promised them to Ingrit if he answered correctly, but, he went on, if he answered incorrectly, he would never let Ingrit eat again and he would never let his body rest untroubled.

After a while the story quickly came babbling out of the terrified Watutsi. The story was, that although the Watutsi were a fairly small tribe in number, they were considered to be of high office amongst those other tribes in Africa, mainly because of their great height, but recently their lordship over the other tribes had been claimed by a new tribe that had come from the south. These new warriors wore lions' tails and were very fierce in battle. The chiefs and elders of the Watutsi people had sent an envoy to the black witch of Mutluc who had told them that their gods needed the great gods to the north in order to defeat this new menace from the south.

So the grave of a Pharaoh had been robbed and the body of the Pharaoh was to be taken with its treasure to the black witch of Mutluc, so that was where they would have to search. They then let Ingrit eat the refreshments that Buryl had brought in whilst they talked in hushed whispers at the end of the room, so as not to be overheard. Nem was all in favour of setting off immediately for the Watutsi homeland but Thylux was more cautious and insisted that they should use the advantage that they already had gained and take Ingrit with them as a prisoner. He said that he was quite confident that Ingrit posed no immediate threat to any of them and that his little added weight in their small boat would not slow them down at all. He said in fact it would be a great advantage to them to have him as a guide and a possible ally. Buryl was surprised at this, as indeed was

Nem. When both young men spoke of their surprise to Thylux he said, 'You could see it in his eyes, we are dealing with a very primitive culture here. He was as afraid of this black witch of Mutluc as he was of you, my prince.'

It was thus decided that they would take Ingrit with them on their journey south. However, although Ingrit was resigned to his fate, he did appeal to them that they accompany him back to his own band of warriors who had come to trade so that he could appoint a new chief in his absence and explain that he had to journey back with these huge men from great Egypt.

It was so that Thylux and Prince Nem of Egypt escorted Ingrit back to where the Watutsi tribesmen were encamped just outside Khartoum, to the south of the city. They had left Buryl behind to re-provision their small boat for an early start in the morning. They found the Watutsi camp and upon entry were challenged by a guard who looked terrified at the prospect of fighting off Thylux. The guard was greatly relieved when he saw Ingrit and quickly stood aside for the three men to pass. Ingrit seemed almost grateful to be returning home, and informed his men that he had agreed to take these huge men from great Egypt back south along the great river to the Watutsi homeland, where they were to meet with the chiefs and elders of the Watutsi tribe and would help in the fight against the warriors from the south. Although this was not quite true, he had discussed it with Thylux if he could use that excuse beforehand, as it had seemed to be the most sensible suggestion. Apart from that, Thylux needed a reason to maintain his pride. The Watutsi warriors would then seem more grateful to the men from great Egypt.

Ingrit then pulled one of the strange feathers from his head, gave it to another man and said, 'I now appoint you in command of this band, and it is your duty to trade as best you can the goods that we have brought up with us.' He then wheeled sharply around and accompanied by his two Egyptian guards, left the Watutsi camp.

They journeyed back to the tavern to find that Buryl had finished provisioning the ship for an early start in the morning. So they went into the tavern for the night, making sure that one of them was awake whilst the other two slept so that they could keep a watchful eye over Ingrit in case he attempted to run away.

When Nem finally drifted off to sleep, his dreams were haunted by the thought of the black witch of Mutluc, who he was sure he had to meet in mortal combat. He woke in a sweat as he was roused by Thylux in the pearly grey of the African dawn. Without even stopping for breakfast, they boarded their small ship and rowed south to meet their fate or to meet what fate had in store for them.

Chapter Nine

They had not been rowing for more than twenty minutes when the breeze from the north once more sprang up, rippling the waters of the smooth river. So they unfurled their sail and continued their journey southward. Moving under sail was an entirely new experience for Ingrit, as he had never seen a sailing vessel before and to him it seemed as if they moved across the water by magic. He was still very wary and cautious of Nem, so he stayed nearer to Thylux. As they journeyed southward, eating wheat cakes for breakfast, Ingrit loosened up and began to tell Thylux what lay ahead of them in the river. He explained that they could go for three days before they came to the first cataract, but that they had to be very cautious about the animals that used the river. Thylux told him that they were experienced boatmen and knew all about the river horse and the crocodile. A few miles further on, Nem, who was standing in the bows, called back to Thylux to steer the ship closer to the west bank as he had seen some large river carp. Nem and Buryl grabbed their fishing spears and before long there were five large fish flopping about in the boat. They then moored the boat beside some trees that over-hung the river and quickly stepped ashore bringing their freshly caught fish, which Nem gutted and cut into strips while Buryl gathered wood for a fire. Whilst the young men were busy with this duty Thylux showed Ingrit how to stow everything in the boat, refold the sail and make everything secure. They then joined the young men on the river bank where Buryl and Nem were cooking strips of fish in olive oil with some herbs and in another pot were boiling some roots, which Buryl had bought in Khartoum. Very soon they all sat round and ate a very tasty lunch of fried carp with some small carrots and small potatoes.

As Thylux and Ingrit were clearing up after the meal, the rest of the carp was hanging on the low branches of the tree drying in the sun and the smoke from the grass that the young men had heaped on the fire for that very purpose. Knowing it would take quite a while before the finished fish strips could be stowed away in the boat, Nem and Buryl had gone for a swim in the river after checking that there were no crocodiles in the area. Watching the two young men swim powerfully up and down, Thylux lay back relaxing in the hot sun but was suddenly brought to his feet by the urgent calls of Ingrit. Ingrit shouted and pointed to the trees that hung above the river and suddenly Thylux saw what he was gibbering about. A huge water python of well over twenty feet had been curled up in the tree, but was now driven down from the tree by the smoke and at that moment fell into the water within a few cubits of Nem and Buryl. Thylux grabbed his sword and charged into the water, but before long all three men were floundering around amidst coils of the great snake that was trying to crush the very air out of them. Each one of them was desperately trying to loosen the python's grip on his own body whilst trying to find the python's head so that they could try to beat it with a rock, or so Thylux could chop its head off. The snake seemed to be aware of their intentions and kept its head out of their way, and even Thylux was beginning to tire and was half drowned by constantly being dragged underwater, when, all of a sudden, they were all amazed and very relieved when the coils of the snake loosened their grip and floated free. Coughing and spluttering the three men dragged themselves ashore to see

that Ingrit had saved their lives by smashing a huge stone
on to the head of the giant snake.

After resting for a few minutes, to recover their breath,
they all heartily thanked Ingrit, shook him by the hand and
slapped him on the back. Nem told him that he was not the
old and dead Pharaoh come back to life again and removed
his gold and silver bracelets to show that they were orna-
ments and not part of his arms, which made Ingrit smile
warmly at him. They were soon under way again, sailing
further into the south. They had noticed that there were
more trees now and the desert had given way to broken
plains with outcrops of rocks where they occasionally saw
some small gazelles and amongst the thorn trees there were
large colonies of nesting birds.

All that day and the next they journeyed south, but they
noticed that the water very gradually became faster and
faster, and soon they heard the roar of the waterfall. Ingrit
said to Thylux that they had journeyed far faster than he
had expected and that they had reached this cataract more
swiftly than he had expected. They moored the boat at the
base of the fall, which seemed to stretch on above them for
a long distance. Leaving the boat at the base of the fall, they

climbed up and realised that the first part of the waterfall was not too high, but was a continuous drop and that there was another fairly calm stretch before the water again whirled and hissed as it came tumbling down from the rocks above, but, even then, its descent was fairly gradual and the river was fairly wide. Unfortunately, apart from around the first stretch where there was the continuous fall, there seemed to be no easy route on which to carry the boat – so, after a discussion, the four of them carried the small boat around the first fall and relaunched it into the river. To Nem and Buryl's surprise, and to Thylux's pleasure, Ingrit appeared to be far stronger than he looked and insisted on carrying his equal share. It was obviously a far

heavier weight than he normally would have attempted to carry, but he felt he had to prove his worth.

Once they had relaunched the boat with the tall Watutsi chief manning the tiller, they threw three ropes out, one either side that went to Nem and Buryl and one in front that went to Thylux. All three of them ploughed their way through the rapids, occasionally standing on firm ground and pulling with all their weight and strength, but some-times swimming against the current and mostly wading knee deep in swirling water, whilst they gradually pulled the boat up the long rapids. They had to pause occasionally for a brief rest, but finally, after a good three hours straining and tugging at the wet ropes, which caused blistering on their hands, they reached the top and saw a whole new landscape in front of them.

The river valley was more pronounced here; the river banks were what had been vast grassy plains which had now dried to a golden tan in the hot African sun. The plains were scattered with groups of trees that mainly had turned into thorns and scrub because of the long, dry hot season and because of the many animals that browsed and grazed on the leaves. Looking around, these northern strangers were amazed at the variety of wildlife, many of which they knew, such as the baboons that chattered down at them from the rocks and the treetops, some of the antelope that ran over the slopes and they saw some of the wildebeest which they had seen in Sudan. But they were all amazed when they saw the long-necked giraffes and the boldly striped zebras that occasionally showed their whereabouts.

After resting to regain their strength, they boarded the boat again and to their delight the wind still blew from the north allowing them to sail on. The three Egyptian men sat and looked in awe as Ingrit described the animals that they saw and pointed out new animals that were camouflaged. They were hidden until you realised what they were. They continued their journey until the sun almost set and then they moored their boat and sat around a campfire. Ingrit told them that they either had to make a thorn fence around their camp, or that they must keep the fire well stocked because of the lions and hyenas, which they would occasionally hear growling and grunting in the night.

Indeed that first night they all had trouble trying to sleep because of the night noises that often chilled the blood.

They awoke as the sun rose alarmingly quickly into the sky, which soon dried any slight moisture that had formed in the night. Chewing handfuls of smoked fish and wheat cakes which they washed down with their last supplies of wine, they boarded the boat and moved off under the slight breeze that was still blowing from the north. However, the breeze gradually died away and they had to use the oars again, but fortunately the current was not strong and they made good progress. Occasionally they saw large forests where there were many animals jumping around in the branches and occasionally they saw areas where the trees had been torn out of the ground and wondered what had happened to them. But one of the most amazing trees of all, which none of the Northerners had ever seen, was the giant baobab tree which, as Nem said, looked as if it were growing upside down.

As they went further south the river went towards the east and they heard from far away a long trumpeting call. The very earth seemed to shake along the river bank and suddenly they saw a huge herd of elephants moving over the big plain. Having never seen an elephant before, they were truly amazed at the size of these animals and at the great long white teeth that curved out of their mouths. Ingrit explained that these teeth were only used for fighting or for splitting the trees that they uprooted by knocking them down in order to eat some of the sweet leaves that only grew at the top or to get at the soft bark which they levered off with those long curved white teeth. Thylux asked Ingrit how they ever hunted them and Ingrit said that they very seldom did unless they caught one on its own and they could force it into a trap or over a cliff. They took the teeth off the animals which had died and traded them to be used as pitchers or for carving.

Once again they made a camp for the night, but this time they made a small semi-circle of thorns that formed a fence against the creatures of the night and generally they spent a far quieter night and slept better than they had on the previous night, although they were still rudely awoken by the roar of a lion that, although Ingrit told them was quite a distance away, sounded as if it was just the other side of the fence. The next morning they awoke to find that the fence on the north side was gradually moving in towards them. They hastily wound up their belongings and got into the boat and had just moved off into the river when they saw what was moving the hedge. There were two great beasts, not quite as large as elephants, but a similar grey, leathery colour with large horns on their noses. This animal, Ingrit said, was a rhinoceros – the toughest beast that they had ever seen and were truly perplexed when Ingrit said they occasionally hunted them for the horn, which was said to have magical properties.

Chapter Ten

All that day and the next they travelled peacefully along the river, pushed along by the light breeze and occasionally using the oars to move them even further south. Then, towards evening, they saw a tribe of black warriors alongside the river bank, who appeared very hostile, shooting arrows from their small bows. But fortunately they were well away from the bank and the arrows fell a long way short of their mark because the bows that these primitive people used were not powerful enough to send their arrows – which were crudely made – a great distance. Nem lifted his own bow and arrows and sent a warning shot whistling over their heads where it thumped into a tree. Realising that this strange craft with the strange large, warriors, who had very powerful weapons, could easily outmatch them, the people disappeared into the grasslands and woods. All this time Ingrit had been lying down, resting in the boat so had therefore not been seen by the black warriors on the bank and when Nem laughingly told him about what had happened he sat up with surprise and said that they sounded like the Hutoo tribe, who were found to the immediate north of his own country. So he had a close look around at where they were and instructed Thylux to steer towards the left bank where the water was flowing a little quicker. Before very long they saw large sandbanks on the right of the river on which the ever-present Nile crocodiles were basking in the sunshine. Ingrit said that this was a very dangerous stretch of the river, because a little further on the river widened but became more shallow which meant that it was often used by large herds of elephant and bison to cross the river.

Buryl, who had been listening very carefully, was about to ask what a bison was when he heard a huge splash and saw an animal which was as large as an ox, but which had enormous horns sticking out of its broad forehead, jump into the river as if it were going to attack the boat. Fortunately, Thylux saw it in time and handed the tiller to Ingrit as he reached down for his large spear which he sent whistling through the air striking the beast on its shoulder. The bison bellowed loudly as it staggered and fell in the water with blood gushing out of the wound that the spear had made. To their amazement there were slithering noises and quiet splashes as the crocodiles smelt the blood in the water and slid off the sandbanks and headed for the commotion in the water. Buryl and Nem grabbed the oars and pulled the boat away from the thrashing beast in the river and as they were doing so they saw the long, evil shapes of the crocodiles gliding swiftly under the boat towards the commotion in the water. Within seconds it seemed that the beast, which was now attempting to drag itself out of the water, was caught by many crocodiles and was swiftly dragged under the water where it was held until it drowned, then torn to pieces.

Thylux indicated a point nearer the bank from which the beast had been dragged underwater, as he saw his spear had half sunk into the river, weighed down by its large bronze head. Keeping well away from the rest of the commotion, which had now drifted towards the middle of the river, they rowed back towards the eastern bank where Thylux managed to retrieve his spear. Ingrit then explained that water buffalo, or bison as he had called it, were one of the few animals who were not afraid of crocodiles. However, any wounded animal was in great danger from crocodiles as they went into a frenzy, driven crazy by the smell of blood.

They rowed on southwards as the wind had dropped and it was now oppressively hot. A little further on, Ingrit ordered Thylux to pull over to the east bank as they were nearing another waterfall. He said that this was not a long or steep fall and that once they entered his own kingdom they would be amongst friends and they began, as previously, pulling the boat up the rapids and were surprised at how quickly they managed the job. Thylux said to Nem that he thought they were all still a bit wary about being in the river after seeing the large bison torn to pieces by the crocodiles, so, without thinking about it, they tried to get the job done as quickly as possible. Shortly after leaving the top of the waterfall they came to a village, set well above the river bank made of circular mud huts with thatched roofs, and where the people from the village waved at Ingrit, making them feel safe, so they moored for the night. They were invited to dinner with the village chief because Ingrit was an old friend of his.

All three of the Egyptians wore their full war gear as they walked through the village with Ingrit. They obviously attracted a great deal of attention, and although most of the Watutsi people in the village were tall, they were not as big as the three men from Egypt who looked most impressive and ferocious in their finery. They stopped outside the chief's hut, where the chief was making room for them by ushering out his wives, children and animals, much to Nem's surprise. When they entered the hut, all three soldiers gagged at the foul stench that came from animal droppings, a lot of human bodies in close confinement and the rancid smell of what was cooking, but they steeled themselves against the stench, as they didn't want to appear rude. They squatted down on rush mats which were hastily produced and the Watutsi chief asked how he could help them, as they were friendly with Ingrit, who was also a relative from one of his marriages.

Without preamble Thylux said, 'We have come to your country in search of a long-dead king whose body was stolen from its resting place, along with many treasures. We have been told by Ingrit that people from your country have stolen what belongs to great Egypt and it is very important to us to have the old king back along with his treasure.'

The chieftain glanced at Ingrit who nodded his head in agreement, and the chief said that these objects were now in their country, but they had been told to bring them here to help in their battle against a tribe from the south.

'But how can a dead king help your battle?' said Prince Nem of Egypt. 'That is what none of us can understand. It was my grandfather's body that was stolen and he is now a god, so we have to retrieve his body and his treasures, otherwise harm may come to our own country.'

The chieftain said the whole story was something that was beyond his control, as all the chiefs and elders of the tribes had sent an envoy to their gods, who spoke through the black witch of Mutluc, so it was a matter for the gods to protect themselves. Thylux was pretty annoyed at being dismissed in such an offhand manner and leapt to his feet, put his hand to the hilt of his sword and demanded that he be taken to this black witch. Prince Nem stood up beside him, with Buryl behind.

Nem took one pace forward and said, 'I am of the bloodline, and therefore I can speak for my ancestors and for my land. I am not scared of any witch as I will soon be a god myself.' He found that he had spoken these words without thinking, and realised that he was shaking as he spoke, partly out of anger, but mainly out of terror.

All three marched out of the hut and refilled their lungs with great gasps of fresh air. Very soon afterwards Ingrit came out of the hut and said, 'We will have to go to see the main assembly of chiefs before they allow us to go to see the black witch of Mutluc. So we will set off first thing in the morning, but the chief did invite you to dine with him.'

'By the gods,' said Thylux, 'I will not enter that vile smelling hut ever again, let alone eat his rancid muck.' Hastily nodding their agreement, Nem and Buryl set off with Thylux back to the boat, with Ingrit trailing behind them.

When they got their provisions off the boat and were ready to eat, Ingrit, who had joined them, said, 'Our quickest way will now be on foot, so before we go we must haul the boat well above the flood line, because rains will soon come.'

Nem then realised why the village was built high above the water and saw where the previous year's flood level had been as there were small boulders which marked the highest point that the river had reached. So after eating a meal of smoked fish and wheat cakes, they hauled the small boat well above the flood level before securing it to a large mopani tree, from which ironwood came, as the mopani tree was one of the hardest in all Africa. They then settled down for the night, but Nem found he was unable to sleep as his mind wandered, and whenever he closed his eyes he saw weird shapes that he supposed were the black witch of Mutluc.

After a hasty breakfast at first light they followed Ingrit up the track that led over the shoulder of the hill to the east of the river, which Ingrit said swept round in a great arc and had two more waterfalls before it came to the citadel where the Watutsi chiefs met. As they went up the track, the sun was only just beginning to show over the edge of the hills to the east and cast long shadows before them. They followed Ingrit in single file, with Nem close behind Ingrit, followed by Buryl and Thylux bringing up the rear. Without warning there was a flurry in the grass to Ingrit's left as a leopard, emerging from the foliage, leapt up at him. He froze in surprise, as leopards normally only hunt by night, and would have been badly mauled by the big cat, but was hugely grateful that its leap had been cut short in mid-flight by Nem's spear, which had not only penetrated the throat but had come out of the back of its neck.

Ingrit bowed down on to one knee before Nem and said, 'I am greatly in your debt, my lord, for indeed you saved my life.'

Nem said, 'I am not your lord, and after all you saved us during the battle with the river python and that is what friendship is all about.'

After a short rest, to help them regain their composure and for the sun to warm up the land, they set off again in a long, swinging trot that covered the ground very quickly, yet with surprisingly little effort.

Keeping in formation, they continued at that pace for hours and then rested under the shade of some trees whilst the sun was high in the sky and burnt down with incredible heat.

'How far is this citadel?' asked Nem and Thylux indicated that it was at least two days' march away. They set off again in the early afternoon, covering the rocky ground very quickly, the pathway occasionally dropping down amongst the trees and the savannah, but mainly kept them on slightly higher ground.

In the heat of the late afternoon, when it was very oppressive and they were sweating profusely, the trail moved up the hills into a low saddle between two higher peaks. At the brow of the hill they paused to look before them. They saw another long line of low hills before them and then caught sight of the river as it turned back towards the east in the far distance. Ingrit, who was used to travelling at this pace, said that there was a small settlement in the next line of hills, so that was where they must get to before nightfall, although they were all rather tired. As their water flasks were empty and they realised that they were all still very thirsty after the long forced march, Ingrit told them to wait while he climbed over a few boulders where a large cactus plant was growing. Using his long dagger he sliced off the bottom section of the cactus which he then cut into sections and gave each of them a section to suck. It was surprisingly moist, beneath its leathery spiny exterior, and full of nutritious fluid that soon restored their strength. They set off again at the same swinging trot and it was not too long before they reached the small settlement, which came into view just as the sun was sinking into the west. The sun sank slowly and all of a sudden it was night time again as in that area, where the sun was almost overhead at midday, there was hardly any twilight when the sun disappeared behind the hills. This was another Watutsi settlement, and somehow people knew of their coming and they found that a hut had already been cleared out for their arrival, and that some food was already prepared for them.

Ingrit said, 'In the morning you will be able to see our destination, because from here it is not far to the high place where the council sits, and from there only a few miles to the holy caves of Mutluc.'

This last name was spoken with great reverence and Nem wondered just what lay in store for him.

They soon fell into an exhausted sleep but were awoken about midnight when they heard a weird howling in the night. Nem saw that his companions were awake, and both looked up startled by the sound, but Ingrit had his face turned away from Nem so that Nem thought he was still asleep.

When he moved closer and put an arm on Ingrit's shoulder to gently wake him he realised that the tall slim Watutsi, who had shown no great fear when he was charged by the leopard or indeed when he had killed the great python, was shivering with his eyes wide open and he muttered, 'That was the black witch summoning the dead.'

Try as he might, Nem could get no further information from Ingrit, and lay for the rest of the night waiting for the dawn and the terrors of the next day, when he must meet this witch.

Chapter Eleven

The dawn eventually came, grey and very humid. The air was very rank in the hut so they moved outside and saw that the sky was still dark with heavy cloud. Although it was very early in the morning they were very hot and there seemed to be no air to breathe. They were given some wheat cakes for breakfast, which was washed down with dark Watutsi beer, which didn't seem to quench their thirst. But there now seemed a terrible urgency, so they hastily moved on towards a low hill on which stood a massive stone structure which Ingrit pointed out was the high place where the chiefs and elders met for gatherings. Walking now at a more reasonable pace, they approached the building and saw that there were other parties making their way to the oldest stone building. As they drew closer and closer it looked more and more like an enormous termites' nest, as it was made of brown clay bricks that were crudely fashioned and jointed with slightly redder clay which had been used as the mortar. Ingrit told them that this building had not been made by the Watutsi tribe, but was made by the old people of whom the black witch was the last to remain.

They entered the gates to this citadel and found that the doors had tall spearmen guarding them. Here they were told to leave their weapons and reluctantly agreed when Ingrit told them that this was done because it was a holy place and no one was allowed to enter with any form of war gear. There were many chiefs already gathered in the large central open chamber and others were still coming in. A lot of the other chiefs welcomed Ingrit and the three men from Egypt. Most of the men in the gathering wore chieftain's ostrich feathers, like Ingrit, but there were some very old men who wore necklaces made of bones, and Ingrit told Nem that they were human bones and these were the old witch-doctors who spoke with the witch and with the gods. The general hubbub died down as one of these old men rose to his feet and said that the Zulu tribe were massing on their southern border and were ready to strike and that despite the witch's spells to bring down a god from the north with his treasure, they did not realise how or why it would help them in the coming battle.

At this point Nem strode forth and said, 'I am Prince Nementhoteptha Pthah Akron, next in line to the throne of Egypt. This god is my grandfather, both he and his treasure belong in my country and it is only in that country where they can work their magic against armies of men.' He then waited whilst his words were translated and everyone understood him, and he then said in almost a shout, 'I demand that you return these treasures to great Egypt – that is why we are here.'

A great hush fell over the crowds and it was then that one of the witch-doctors spoke, and he said, 'We are oath bound not to return the treasures until commanded by the black witch.'

'Then where is this black witch?' shouted Nem, 'for she has threatened my own country and my own bloodline by stealing these treasures.'

After a long pause a spokesman for the witch doctors said, 'We cannot possibly ask her. You yourself must ask the black witch.'

Nem said, 'I demand to go now!' But the witch-doctor refused as he said, 'No one can take you, for we must fight our enemy the Zulu.'

There was then a long silence which was eventually broken by Thylux as he clapped his hands together to draw attention to himself, 'If you will take Nem to see the black witch, Buryl and I will fight for you against your enemy!' This had been said so commandingly that it was accepted as an order rather than a compromise. The meeting was then over and the three men from Egypt split company, each wishing the other good fortune. It was decided that two of the witch-doctors would accompany Nem, whilst all of the chiefs gathered together to discuss how they would face battle against the Zulus.

The chiefs were already discussing how the tribes should line up when Thylux halted them all and said, 'Do any of you know the Zulu strategy and way of fighting?' There was a long silence as none of the Watutsi had ever faced the Zulu warriors.

Thylux then said, 'Do they not fight in the form of the buffalo's horns?' Thylux asked this question because on his last campaign he had heard rumours of the Zulus and how they always won their victories by a certain tactic.

As no man came forward he said, 'Listen to me and I will lead your army into certain victory.' He looked so proud and massive a man amongst the tall Watutsi tribal chiefs, and they had all heard great stories of how the Egyptian army was invincible, so they quickly agreed to Thylux's offer.

Thylux picked up a stick, and whilst the Watutsi chiefs gathered around him, he drew in the sand the shape of two buffalo horns and two oblong square boxes in between the horns.

'This, I believe, is how the Zulu strategy works – the head moves forward.' And he showed with arrows how the two centre oblongs moved forward. He then said, 'But this is only a feint and then they will quickly withdraw so that your army will pursue them. At the same time the two horns on either side will move forward to outflank your army and the head will then move forward again crushing you against the encircling horns.' He waited to allow this to sink in and then said, 'The secret is not to be drawn in and to have our side flanks strengthened against the encircling horns. If we do not get drawn in, when their head feints and retreats, their horns will have to move further to encircle us, drawing strength from the head. To increase this effect we could also retreat slowly *en masse*, and then, when their head attacks they will have to charge over a greater distance and there will be fewer of them as they will have had to reinforce their horns. And at that point we must counter-attack with tremendous force, but leaving our flanks well guarded. That way we can smash through the head between the horns and the two sides will be cut off.'

All the Watutsi chiefs looked at Thylux with awe and knew that their gods had sent them the means by which they could defeat the Zulu menace, and they hastily agreed that Thylux should lead their army. Thylux agreed to this and said that he wanted Buryl in charge of the right flank and their best warrior chieftain in charge of the left flank.

'And I will come up the middle and it is very important that you obey my commands.' They all agreed to this and left the citadel to go down to where their army was assembled.

Meanwhile, Nem had left the citadel with two of the witch-doctors who had introduced themselves as Ostric and Amhar. Apparently Amhar was a full-scale witch-doctor and Ostric was still a novice but just awaiting his coming of age celebration at which he would be inducted into the full witch-doctors' order. Both were striking young men in that they were taller than Nem but very, very skinny, yet surprisingly agile as they seemed to dance along the track rather than walk or run. Nem insisted on wearing his full war gear, despite the fact that Amhar told him he must not carry any weapon within the boundaries of Mutluc. Nem had no such intention – he felt naked without his sword and shield, spear and bow, and he thought that he was going into the heart of his enemy's territory and he knew that it would take all his courage to face the witch. They journeyed east towards the great river and reached the water just before it came crashing down another waterfall. Amhar and Ostric kept walking along the bank toward the waterfall, where there seemed to be no way forward but much to Nem's surprise, Amhar, who was in front, ducked beneath some green bushes and the spray from the waterfall hid him, but his voice clearly called after him, 'Follow me, just the way I came.' Ostric and Nem did exactly the same and much to Nem's surprise they came out behind the waterfall into what was a fairly dry recess, yet it was fairly light because the light shone through the great gush of water as it fell over the rocks behind them. Amhar turned to Ostric and told him that as he was only a novice he should come no further but should stay here on guard, whilst Amhar would take Nem to the inner sanctum of Mutluc.

Nem wondered what his friends were doing at that very minute but was soon brought out of his thoughts by a hideous wailing that seemed to come from deep inside the very earth and even drowned out the sound of the waterfall. Amhar suggested that Nem leave his weapons where they were, but Nem, who had tightened his grip upon his spear and had one hand on his sword hilt, shook his head in a very defiant gesture. Amhar tried to insist but Nem just held his spear at arm's length towards the tall, skinny Watutsi and commanded him to lead on. Amhar turned on his heel and lead Nem to the back of the cave, where a small lamp was lit. Here the roof of the cave was only about four feet above the floor so that both men had to almost bend double. Amhar had picked up a funnel of rushes which he lit from the lamp to use as torchlight and continued on around the corner towards where the hideous wailing was coming from. The pathway closed in on both sides, although it did become slightly higher and as they shuffled along the floor which was not just messy but seemed to move with insects and snakes which glided over the bats' guano. All of a sudden the wailing ended and there was utter silence and this, Nem thought, was even worse, but still they moved onwards through the living rock where the torchlight flickered over the floor which seemed to move and glisten with a myriad of objects that scuttled out of their way. Without warning the rock seemed to echo to a harsh barking that chilled the very blood, yet still Amhar led Nem forward. The barking stopped as abruptly as it had started. It was then replaced by a growling which seemed to come from every direction and still Amhar went forward. They then came to a wider part where all of a sudden the floor of the cavern disappeared for many hundreds of feet beneath them.

As the growling died away the darkness seemed to deepen and Amhar turned to Nem and said in a hushed whisper, 'I can go no further; from here you must go on alone.'

Nem's heart was pounding in his chest and he looked to where Amhar pointed – a narrow bridge spanned the enormous cleft that disappeared below the torchlight and Nem could barely see across the cavern where three bone crosses were mounted on the wall above a doorway that was guarded on either side by pale wolf-human skulls, which seemed to be leering at Nem. Drawing his sword, which rasped from its sheath, he stepped cautiously and carefully on to the rope bridge which crossed the vast cavern and he gingerly made his way across.

He glanced back to Amhar who saw the beads of sweat on his brow. Amhar said, 'Take heart, lord Nem, do not let your courage fail you now.'

The growling stopped, again to be replaced by the fearful silence that seemed to close in about him, yet as he tightened his grip on his sword and his spear he knew he must enter the evil doorway and so, with his heart pounding very loudly in his ears, he ducked his head through the doorway which led on through a narrow tunnel which continued down and down on a winding path. The darkness seemed to press in on him from all sides, but suddenly there seemed to be a faint, reddish glow in front of him and so he started towards the light. This reddish glow flickered before him and he saw another archway at the end of the passage, where it entered another passage from where the light was coming. All of a sudden there was a spine-chilling shriek which died in a cackle of laughter. Taking his courage in both hands and bracing himself for the evil that lay ahead, he lurched through the doorway.

The sight before his eyes frightened and astonished him as he confronted what must have been the witch of Mutluc. The witch was an old crone of many years, who had a wide toothless grin which seemed to spread from ear to ear beneath a thatch of white hair. There was a large fire behind her which crept up into a chimney which was deep in the recesses of the rock behind her, yet twisting around her skinny arms and legs were two of the most lethal snakes in all of Africa. Two black mambas were wriggling around her body in what seemed a dance of death.

The old crone smiled at Nem and said, 'Do you like my pets? Young prince, come closer so that I can have a good look at you.'

However, seeing the bodies and skeletons that lay in front of him and knowing the danger of these wicked snakes, that could cross a twenty-foot gap in the twinkling of an eye, Nem stood his ground and plucking up his courage he shouted in a defiant voice, 'You old hag, I demand the return of my grandfather's mummy and the treasure that you told your people to steal from his burial chamber.'

There was a long silence after which the witch grinned and said, 'Careful, Prince Nem, my pets do not allow people to give me orders.'

Nem found the witch's voice strangely enchanting and almost did not see one of the mambas sudden strike towards his left leg. Acting purely on instinct he sliced quickly with his sword only to sever the creature's cruel head from its body. The snake's body whirled and twitched a few times, then it lay dead. The witch screamed in rage and hurled the other snake towards Nem but he was ready for this and the snake's open jaws met Nem's spear thrust which came out of the back of the snake's head. He wound the spear around with the snake's body still on the end of it, which struck the old witch as she screamed and jumped back into the fire. The dead snake came off the end of Nem's spear as its body wrapped around the witch and it burnt with a fierce blue, hissing flame as the witch stood in the fire. She then became a living torch as her white hair hissed and burnt with fierce sparks of octerine light as she gasped her last breath and collapsed like a rag doll in the blaze.

Chapter Twelve

Nem stood breathing deeply in the flickering firelight with bones and corpses all around. He shuddered as he realised that although he had killed what he considered was his enemy, he had now to justify his actions to the witch-doctors and he still had to find the missing body of his grandfather and the treasure. He then realised with an inward groan that that was one of his least worries as his two companions had led the Watutsi tribe into a terrible battle. He then fell on his knees half with exhaustion and half in fright, and prayed to his gods to help him in his hour of desperate need. After a few minutes he rose from his knees and realised that the only way forward was to be honest and truthful, and as the stench of the cave and the silence began to crowd in on him, he turned sharply on his heel and retraced his footsteps through the narrow doorway and up along the winding path through the living rock until he came to the chamber where the narrow rope and wood bridge spanned the chasm.

Meanwhile Thylux and Buryl were deep in conversation as they led the Watutsi army that followed the two of them like an enormous snake twisting its way through the low brown hills.

Ingrit kept up beside Thylux and said, 'We have decided who is the best leader to guard the left flank of the army.'

Another chief walked beside Ingrit, who introduced himself as Umtal. Without warning, the hilltop in front of them was crowned by a mass of Zulu warriors who stretched down both sides of the hill and who started their killing chant which started with a low 'Jee, jee.' Then there was a clash as the Zulus rattled their spears against their hide shields. Realising his predicament and knowing that they had just started climbing up the hill, Thylux ordered the whole army to retreat to the other side of a small brook that they had crossed just a few minutes earlier. As they scurried back, the Zulu war chant seemed to grow in intensity behind them, but whilst they were retreating, he ordered his chiefs to take up their previously agreed battle formation, with Buryl commanding his right flank, which he instructed to bend back like a bow, and Umtal in charge of the left flank, where again he turned the edges back.

He then took charge of the central section alongside Ingrit and he shouted, 'The Zulus will charge first through the brook and then retreat whilst their flanks advance.' He went on to shout in a loud voice that their central section would retreat behind the brook as if they were running away. He raised his voice again and said, 'But no one must pursue them – indeed I will chop down the first one of you who steps over the brook.' By this time the killing chant of the Zulus had reached a fever pitch and they were all beginning to advance down the hill, towards the terrified Watutsi front rank.

At this point Thylux stood in front of his first rank wearing his majestic helmet, which made him look really enormous, and his bronze breastplate shone in the afternoon sun that slashed across the hillside. The sun also glinted on his huge spear which he planted firmly in the earth as a challenge to the Zulus as he drew his own sword. The Zulu chant died into a strange silence as they had never seen these lighter-skinned men from the north with their curious body armour, but in order to reinforce their challenge the Zulu witch-doctors came to the fore, chanting and wailing weird incantations whilst rattling handfuls of human bones. The Zulus were then encouraged and started their killing chant again and just started their frontal charge towards the central section of the Watutsi army. The front ranks of the Watutsi were all amazed as the Zulu charge was thrown off balance, as two arrows felled two of the advancing witch-doctors, and within a few seconds two other witch-doctors had met the same fate. Still the Zulus kept up their charge and came across the brook yelling their bloodthirsty chant, but they were not now in an ordered line. Thylux picked up his bow and many arrows, as did Buryl who hastily ran back to take his place at the front of the right flank. The Zulus had encountered bows and arrows before but only small arrows that were fired only a small distance and without great force, so it was first blood to the Watutsis and a great cheer went up from their army.

But the Zulus were by then in a frenzy, driven by their killing chant. Their hide shields clashed against the hide shields of the Watutsi ranks, and they used their short spears in deadly killing thrusts which came above the shields. Thylux had by then removed his spear from the ground, brushed away the leading Zulu shield with a sweep of the blade and rammed the spear head deep into the belly of the advancing Zulu, whilst his own shield cast aside the thrust of the Zulu spear. The fighting was fast and furious for a few moments but the Zulus lost most of their front rank as the Watutsi spearmen following Thylux's lead, rebuffed the Zulu first charge as it came at them. There was a sharp bellow from a bullhorn.

'Stand firm,' said Thylux. As if they had changed their minds because of the severe punishment that Thylux and the first guard of the Watutsi were dishing out, the Zulus started to retreat across the brook. Some of the Watutsi immediately started after them, but checked their step when Thylux bellowed, 'Hold your ground!'

The Zulu attackers retreated but were not followed by the Watutsi, who followed the order Thylux gave to them. Thylux crouched around to see Buryl at the right-hand end of the flank where it started to curve back, and he grinned with satisfaction. He then glanced to his left to see that Umtal was in the identical position to Buryl but on the left flank. Much to his surprise and annoyance, he noticed that the chieftain had moved forward along the right flank which had the effect of allowing the end to straighten up.

He twisted round to Ingrit and said, 'You must send a runner to Umtal and tell him to move back to his original place where our end line must curve back, to ensure that we are not outflanked.'

Ingrit, who had a chain of runners under his command sent two of them to ensure that the order was obeyed. As the Zulu front line retreated, they were very perplexed and very surprised that they were not pursued, but nonetheless kept moving back beyond the brook. Whilst they were retreating, almost inconceivably, their two side battalions were advancing in order to surround the Watutsi. However, at that point Thylux gave the order to move back very slowly yet keeping in formation. In order to stretch out their advancing columns to surround the advancing Watutsi, many of the central second rank had to join the surrounding force. Then the horn blew again and the Zulus stopped in their retreat, turned sharply and attacked once more with ferocity and vehemence, chanting their killing war cry which worked them up into a frenzy. Firstly, they were surprised at how far away the Watutsi front rank now were, and it was not until they splashed through the brook that they realised the Watutsi had moved back quite a long way so they had even further to charge. This had the effect of breaking down the charge into groups who came on at differing speeds.

Thylux grinned with pleasure, and rendered his second rank to charge, after his first rank had stemmed the initial attack, and, as that attack was not so well covered as it should have been, the clash of shields was not a massive crunch but rather a ragged clashing like two turtles fighting.

As the Zulu front line was held up, Thylux swung his broad-bladed spear which neatly decapitated two of the attackers at the same time and bellowed, 'Charge!' The second rank of Watutsi spearmen came screaming forwards, led on by Thylux who penetrated deeper and deeper into the Zulu's central attack formation, as that centre had been weakened to strengthen the encircling Watutsi. Victory was almost in their grasp and Thylux checked his two flanks: on his right Buryl was doing an excellent job in hacking down the Zulu warriors and stopping them from breaking or outflanking his bent-back shield wall. But when he glanced to his left Thylux groaned in horror; Umtal had moved back to the end of his line – their shield wall did not bend back on itself and, as he gazed in sheer disbelief, he saw advancing Zulu warriors outflanking their shield wall which was beginning to fall as Umtal was cut down from behind.

Chapter Fourteen

It was very dark in the cavern, so dark that Nem could not see across the chasm to where he had left Amhar. Furthermore, there seemed to be no glow on the other side of the chasm showing where Amhar was.

'Amhar!' called Nem, but there was no reply. Feeling the darkness close in around him he decided that he must try to get out of the tunnels himself. So, crawling on his knees, he felt for the rope bridge and carefully crept his way over until he could stand up, pressed against the rock on the far side. All his other worries forgotten for the moment, he concentrated on finding the doorway and having discovered it, more by luck than by action, he ducked inside. Now he was totally engulfed in funereal darkness and the horrors of what he had witnessed in the cave of the witch would have driven him mad had it not been for his one overriding passion to get out and back to his fellow warriors, because something made him feel that he was needed. So he pressed on, using his spear in front of him to check for dips and hollows in the ground. Believing that he heard a noise in the omnipresent dark he paused and froze to listen; one of the horrible centipedes crawled over his face, but he managed to remain still as he strained to listen for voices. Yes, there was definitely the murmur of two people talking in front of him and he broke into a shambling run as he turned into the cave at back of the waterfall. There in front of him was Amhar arguing with Ostric.

Both of them wheeled around when they heard Nem coming, and Amhar gazed in amazement and stammered, 'We thought you were dead.'

'Not I,' said Nem, 'it is the black witch of Mutluc and her vile serpents that lie burned horribly to death beyond the chasm.'

Much to Nem's surprise the two witch-doctors fell to their knees and said with great deference, 'Thank the gods that you live, for we were told that we were escorting you to your certain death. As no one knew why the black witch had ordered what she had, as we all feared taking treasure from great Egypt.'

It then became clear to Nem that in some strange way the witch had summoned the only people who could possibly save them from the Zulu menace, but again Nem got this nagging feeling at the back of his mind telling him that he must find his friends.

He said to Amhar and Ostric, 'Quick, lead me to the place of the battle, for I know I am needed.' So they set off at a fast-paced trot which they kept up for over an hour before they came to the battlefield.

Thylux's groan of despair was soon dispelled as a spear flew threw the air and skewered the Zulu warrior, he who had killed Umtal from the rear. The rest of the Zulus who had outflanked the left side of the Watutsi army wheeled around to face a new challenge coming as if from nowhere. Prince Nem engaged the enemy, cutting down two Zulus at each side of him which gave heart to the Watutsi left flank and they rallied to crush the outflanking Zulus.

Thylux stood transfixed for almost too long and he suddenly felt his spear jerked to the side and only half escaped the blow from the mighty war axe which was wielded by a grim-looking attacker. Luckily, most of the blow was deflected by his breastplate, but his left shoulder was still badly wounded and his left arm was now soaked in his own blood. This annoyed him greatly as he had not been wounded to such a degree for a long time. So, drawing his own sword, he charged at the opponents and cut down three, before the ranks in front of him broke. They had broken through the Zulu army, which was snapped in two, and in a dramatic break the Zulus were suddenly retreating. He called for his men to stand firm and not to follow as they had already won the day.

All the chiefs gathered around Thylux, who immediately told them to stop their men from looting the dead Zulu warriors.

'There is nothing worse than despoiling the dead. After they have honoured themselves in battle, they should be allowed to go to their gods in their full glory.'

This was said with such dignity and force that the Watutsi chieftains immediately sent such an order to their men.

Presently Buryl came up to Thylux and grinned, then said, 'Who had the audacity to bite your shoulder?'

Thylux glanced at the wound and shrugged, 'It must have been a mosquito who bit me before I flicked it away,' and he glanced at Buryl who had lost the little finger of his left hand, and jokingly said, 'At least I didn't give them any part of my body.'

A slightly embarrassed Buryl said, 'Well, I swapped it for this hand,' and he held up a severed hand which was covered in gold rings. As both soldiers were grinning and talking about the victory they had just won, Nem came into view.

'And what kept you, my prince?' said Thylux. 'You almost missed all the fun.' But Nem could not be so lighthearted, as his mind was churning with worries.

'Oh, Thylux,' he said, 'I have slaughtered the black witch, we have just won the battle for them and they still have our treasure and my grandfather's body, so we seem to

have got into a hopeless situation. Surely they could easily
kill us off now as there is no proof that we ever got this far.'

'Oh, Nem,' said Thylux, 'what little faith you have in
soldiers. Although they fight for different chieftains they
are normally honourable people. Just wait and see, everything will work out.'

The Watutsis insisted on carrying the three battle-weary
men from the north back to the citadel, cheering and
singing of their bravery as they went. They were then
placed in a position of honour in front of the Watutsi chiefs
and elders.

It was Ingrit who spoke and he said, 'We owe you a great
debt, for you have done what we thought was impossible.
Indeed, the black witch told us the only way to bring you
here, so there was a purpose behind the robbery. We will
now gladly return your treasure; indeed, it is under the very
floor that you stand upon.'

He waved away their thanks and told them, 'You are
obviously worried about killing the black witch but that was
her purpose all along. The old religion will not die but a
young witch, who has been specially trained, will become
the tribe's spiritual leader. But now you must rest, your
wounds will be treated by our doctors and then we will
discuss how to return everything to Egypt to whom it
belongs.'

They were all struck dumb by this unexpected kindness
and they all succumbed to the offer of food for they had so
long seemed to be on meagre rations. Ingrit led them from
the citadel to a nearby tent, which was more of a semicir-
cular strange wooden shape. They therefore agreed to be
pampered by the Watutsis and spent a few quiet days just
wondering about how well everything had worked out.
Thylux, although he insisted that he was unhurt, eventually
agreed to have his wound dressed with a poultice that the
witch-doctors made up and Buryl had his finger stump

bound up. So there was plenty of extravagant food brought forward and the evening was spent in merrymaking whilst bards and poets sung of their glories.

Just at the end of the feast Ingrit came over and addressed all three and said, 'Tomorrow we will show you all that we stole and discuss how we can return it to its rightful place in great Egypt,' and they all marvelled at this generosity and kindness.

The following morning, after they had slept for a long time as they had been very weary, they were washed by servants and dressed in fine Watutsi robes whilst their own clothes were being washed and their weapons cleaned. Ingrit then led them back to the citadel and to an underground door in which they found the dead Pharaoh, who was intact, with a fine flax robe draped over the death mask. They counted their store of treasury chests in all the rooms and agreed that there were twenty-one, the exact number that had been stolen.

Ingrit said, 'You are probably wondering how you can get these treasures back to Egypt, for obviously your fine little boat is not capable of carrying all these heavy chests of gold and jewels.'

He went on to say that the chiefs and elders had convened a council after last night's party and Ingrit told them that the basic plan was as follows. They would make three or four large rafts cut from the large trees in the forests to the east on which the treasures could be secured and could then be floated down the river on its annual flood which was only a couple of weeks away. As he said this, a small rainstorm started as if to emphasise that the rains were starting at long last. However, Nem had not slept very well as he had been worried about killing the black witch, who after all had been the strange counsellor to the Watutsi tribe.

So he turned to Ingrit and said, 'How will you now be sure that you obey the will of your gods as you no longer have an intermediary to ask?'

Ingrit smiled, and put his arm around Nem's shoulders and he said, 'In truth, lord prince, you did us a favour. The witches of Mutluc renew themselves from their own holy order and the witch that you killed was possibly the most brutal within living memory. Indeed, she normally killed one or more of our envoys which she considered just payment for summoning the gods to our aid. This last episode really shows how devious she was, because only with your treasure to recover could we ensure your assistance.'

Nem was intensely grateful to hear these words because he felt that his actions in the caves of Mutluc had been sacrilege to the Watutsi gods. So it was as if a great burden had been lifted from his shoulders.

Thylux then interrupted and said, 'Surely if we all work together on the rafts we can finish them in under two weeks.' He said this because he was impatient to get home as he had a nagging sensation that the Hittite empire would strike at Egypt before the new year's flood.

'Perhaps we can,' said Ingrit, 'but the wood will have to be carried from the forests to the east, so we must waste no further time in considering just how. We will do it, indeed I think you seem to be better boat builders, having more than our amount of boat travel experience. You will have one hundred men under your command. Today I will take you to the forest to show you what trees to cut.'

Chapter Fifteen

And so it was that a few hours later, Ingrit led the three men from Egypt back towards the Nile where a small craft was waiting to paddle them across. After crossing the bright river once more they set off, using the ground-eating loping trot which they had used before. And shortly afterwards, they crossed the river valley to see another line of low hills in the middle distance which were far greener than anything they had yet seen. Ingrit pointed out that the hills were covered with trees and in this part of the country there was often a lot of rain every day which kept the trees looking green, but warned them that in the hills there were also the great apes, that normally kept their distance as they did not like men but were ferocious and very strong.

'So if you see any of them be careful not to arouse them, but move quietly away,' said Ingrit.

Nem asked him if they were the animals from which Ingrit's necklace was made.

Ingrit answered him whilst fondling the necklace, 'Yes, I killed this animal when I was thirteen summers old, and I was then declared to have attained manhood.'

They then set off again and before long reached the first crop of trees. These trees were far larger than anything that the Egyptians had ever seen before and Ingrit said that they were very hard wood and quite difficult to cut, but when dry floated well enough and made a very secure raft when they were bound together.

Buryl, who had seen large trees before in his homeland, said that he had been giving the whole matter of building the rafts a lot of thought. 'If we select the right trees, we can make two narrow hulls the lengths of three trees each and bind them in the thick skin of the baobab tree, which floats easily and is very springy, and then form a lattice work of split bamboo that will hold the two main sections parallel.'

He drew what the raft would look like when finished with the blade of his dagger in the soft earth. 'By doing it this way,' he said, (little knowing that he was designing the first catamaran known to mankind), it will mean that we will not have to cut and carry so many great logs. They all looked in wonder at the sketch that Buryl had made and all of them agreed that it was worth a try, as in the long run it would save a lot of time.

So as they walked into the forest they marked with a deep cross cut into the wood with their swords which of the large trees they wanted. These were all tall trees whose girth was approximately the full span of one person.

Thylux said they would have to make Buryl their chief boat builder. 'So tell us how many of these trees to cut down, so that they can be brought down to the river bank and you will then have to tell us how many of the bamboo poles to bring.'

So it was decided and about thirty trees were marked with the cross.

'Where is the best place to get the bamboo from?' asked Thylux.

Ingrit pointed to the far side of the large hill. He said, 'But we must be cautious, because the bamboo is a food source for the great apes.' He looked at the dying rays of the sun as it sank behind the hills in the west and said, 'I can show you but it will mean that we will have to camp out for the night.'

After a brief discussion, they decided that this was the best idea, so they made a camp, cutting a small shelter in case it rained and whilst Thylux and Ingrit were finishing the camp and collecting wood for a fire, Nem and Buryl took up their bows and arrows in order to find some food to cook for supper.

Nem said that at the edge of the forest he had seen some tracks that were indicative of those guinea fowl that live all over the forest, which were quite easy to catch and kill as they spend a lot of time walking on the ground pecking at the earth. Sure enough, they encountered some guinea fowl tracks and with drawn bows they quietly stalked their prey down the track that led to a clearing in which quite a few of these plump birds were pecking at the earth.

Signalling to Buryl, Nem turned left so that they were both on one side of the clearing. Each of them sighted along their strange arrows which they let fly, quickly inserting another arrow into the bow which managed to get into the air almost in unison with the thud of the arrow as it hit its target. So they had four dead birds neatly shot through the neck before the rest flew off in panic.

Congratulating themselves and knowing that they would eat well this night, they collected their catch and returned to camp just as the sun was setting. They discussed how many of the bamboo trees they would need whilst they plucked the birds and made supper. And they all enjoyed the roasted guinea fowl which they roasted on spits above the flames of a fire that crackled warmly in the pleasant evening. They all turned in to the shelters that night where Ingrit had heaped lots of ferns which made a comfortable bedding on which they could sleep. There were two shelters, one on ether side of the fire and they crept tiredly to bed, because they all knew that there was another long day ahead of them.

Nem was about to drop off to sleep, after talking to Buryl for a few minutes discussing the day's events, when he was suddenly awakened by a loud but distant wavering cry which ended in a hollow thumping sound. Both he and Buryl sat bolt upright, exchanged glances, were about to speak when the same cry re-echoed through the forest. Crawling out of their shelter, they emerged at the same time that Thylux and Ingrit did. Ingrit threw a large bundle of dry wood on the glowing embers of the fire, before answering questions that the other three fired at him.

Once he had kindled the fire into a bright blaze again he said, 'Yes, my friends, that was one of the great apes, in fact the greatest of them all, the silver back gorilla.' He went on to explain that although they were extremely powerful and frightening creatures, they were also very timid. They would also not come into the camp, unless by accident, so he said, 'Return to your shelters, they will have seen the fire from a long distance as they have very sharp eyesight and will note the position of our camp.'

But they were all wide awake still, their drowsiness forgotten. None of them was keen to go back to try to sleep. Therefore they asked Ingrit question after question about the forest. Ingrit gave honest answers to all the questions but said that there was a lot that the Watutsi did not know about forest life. He went on to say that even further to the east there was a forest with trees that were ten times taller than the ones that they were to cut, and the forest was so dark that the sunshine never reached the earth and everything was seen beneath the green roof of leaves. Prompted by his tales of the large forest and of its people, the little ones as he called them, indicating with his hand that they were only the size of children.

Fascinated by this vastly interesting land, they listened to his stories well into the night until he said, 'I can talk no longer, so now we must sleep.' And so saying, he returned to his shelter, so they all went back and very soon fell into a deep dreamless sleep.

They awoke late in the morning, and so did not stop to gather anything to eat but climbed the hill, turned north-west, over the side and up the next hill to where the bamboo wood lay.

Buryl said, 'We need bamboo lengths of approximately three times my height and also we need the thick bark that we can split to make the lattice floor of the rafts.' He went on to explain that by making everything in this manner they would be able to dismantle the rafts very quickly and roll up the lattice mats so that they could carry the rafts when they came to the huge cataract at the end of the plains. So they split up and each one searched a designated area and marked it with a cross. He cut into the bamboo when he came across one of the correct size.

Nem had wandered further than the others as he was fascinated by the bamboo forest that was shrouded in mists from the frequent rains. Then to his surprise he saw what he thought was a huge monkey cracking open one of the bamboo shoots so that it could lick out the chewy pith inside. Nem stopped in his tracks fascinated by the creature and he did not move for fear of making a noise. Then suddenly his attention was broken as four small black animals broke through the bamboo; these four baby monkeys jumped on to its back and they went into the distance. As they did so, Nem saw that the hair on its back was tinted with silver.

He made his way back to the rest of the party, called the others round and told them what he had seen. Ingrit quickly confirmed that he had seen one of the great silver back gorillas and that it was not really safe to stay in the area if they were around. Buryl only half listened, as he was calculating something in his mind and said that they had probably marked enough of the bamboo poles for the purpose, so they decided to make their way back to the river and gather together the one hundred men they had been promised to help cut the trees, drag them to the river and build the rafts that would carry the treasure home.

They arrived later the same day and before sundown they had gathered together the allotted men who would help them in their task. They decided to journey back the next morning and to split the men into two main companies. The larger company of about sixty men were to be led by Thylux and would cut and drag the huge hardwood trees. The smaller gang of about forty men would be led by Nem and would bring back the bamboo. Ingrit said that the council had decided to give them a further twenty men who had volunteered to help them build the rafts and these men would accompany them on their journey home to Egypt. He said it would be best if these men set up a camp by the river where they would build the rafts under the direction of Buryl as he had the design for the style of building.

So early next morning they set out with the first one hundred men and Ingrit said that they would follow shortly with the other twenty volunteers. Turning left from the citadel they journeyed back to the river where, hopefully, more canoes had been brought along for them to cross the Nile. And so leaving with the men who had ferried them all across the river, to wait for his volunteer helpers, the men led by Thylux and the men led by Nem made their way back to the forest.

It was hard work collecting the trees, although the stone axes that the Watutsis used were surprisingly efficient but the main job was pulling down the trees which caught in the branches of their neighbouring trees. However, the main work was carried out in two days and the bamboo poles were collected very quickly by the Watutsis who worked in gangs and sang as they worked, which Ingrit told

Nem ensured that none of the forest animals came near them, and of course it also cheered along the work which went very quickly. However by now the rains had started in earnest and each day dawned grey and rained and rained for long periods. It was not cold rain but tepid, and after a while they got used to working in the rain which was quite refreshing as it washed off the sweat that they very quickly worked up in the hot steamy jungle. Hauling back the trees to the river was possibly harder than they had imagined. But they soon found that the best way was to cut the branches from the trunks and roll the tree trunks back down the gradually slipping trail to the river, which seemed to be rising as they watched.

Buryl had set up four teams and each team was building a raft, so he was kept very busy going amongst these teams and supervising the work. Within a further two days they had completed all four rafts which they gingerly pushed into the river to see if Buryl's idea really worked. They were all very impressed with the finished results because although the heavy logs were almost submerged in the water, the lattice roll-up floor to the rafts held the logs firmly in place and floated a full hand's span above the river and they realised that the heavy treasure chests could all be secured on to the rafts.

The treasures were then brought down from the citadel, and secured to the rafts; each carried approximately the same load. They were soon ready to leave. Ingrit had discovered the man who had been in charge of the party who stole the treasures, and that man said that he was very keen to return everything that his people had stolen because he felt that that would be the best way to dispel the curse that had fallen on his family. At home, nothing had been going right since they had stolen the treasure, and this he obviously blamed on the curse.

Chapter Sixteen

On the following morning, the whole council of elders and chiefs, with the accompanying witch-doctors, all came down to the bank of the swollen river to wish farewell to the party that was travelling down river back to great Egypt. Amongst the twenty men who had volunteered to accompany the men back to Egypt was Ingrit who was now a very close friend to all the three northerners, and with him the man who had originally led the raiding party that stole the treasure. His name was Umlite and he was the brother of Umtal who had died bravely in the war with the Zulus. Also in the party was Ostric, the man who was a trainee witch-doctor yet still had to finish his training. He was undecided as to what his future would be but simply knew that he felt indebted to Nem, as Nem had killed the black witch of whom he had been truly terrified. The other seventeen volunteers were all good reliable rivermen who were keen to repay the debt that they owed the men from Egypt.

With five men on each raft, one at the prow keeping a lookout for any dangers ahead and two on each side with long paddles with which they could help steer the rather ungainly craft, Thylux, Nem and Buryl were all on the leading raft with Ingrit. Just before they set off the council of chiefs and elders came aboard to say farewell on their journey and once more to thank them for leading the victory against the Zulus.

Thylux graciously accepted their thanks and said that he had been proud to be the general of their army and that they were good fighting men that he would be proud to have in his army, if any wished to come north to Egypt to serve under him. Buryl said the same and that he had made many new friends. However, the greatest thanks came from Nem who said that he perfectly understood their action of raiding the tomb as they were forced into an action that they did not understand and he then went on to pledge that there was now a bond between the people from the Watutsi nation and those from Egypt and should the Watutsi people need help in any battles against warring neighbours they could always call on Egypt particularly if he finally became Pharaoh, as was anticipated. With those final words and many cheers to send them on their way the barges slowly pushed out into the stream where they quickly gathered speed in the fast flowing river and they soon disappeared heading north-west.

Their first port of call was the village where they had left their boat and bearing in mind that it was over a day's march if they kept to the river, they were very amazed when Ingrit said after only a couple of hours travelling that they had better pull over to the east bank, which was now on their right, because the village lay just around the next bend. Everything looked so different as the river had overflowed its normal banks and although it was not raining then, they were travelling beneath a low leaden sky that was threatening heavy rain at any moment. The large rafts were slow and cumbersome to manoeuvre out of the fast current in the middle of the river but fortunately Ingrit had warned them in time. Even so the first craft just ran aground a small distance past the village with the rest of the craft following in close order. Each raft was attached to a short length of stout rope made from split bamboo pith that allowed the barges a certain amount of individual control but kept them in close alignment.

Thylux, Nem and Buryl left the front raft with Ingrit in command and checking that each raft was securely tethered to the bank they walked back to the village to retrieve their boat. At the village, they were delighted to see that the boat had been well looked after and had been re-provisioned for their journey north. And so with many thanks to the chief they ran the boat down to the river which was not far and the ground was slippery so the boat slid easily down into the river. They swiftly boarded the boat and drifted down with the current to where the barges were moored. As their boat was twice as fast as the barges they thought it would be prudent to secure their stern with a long line to the leading raft and then set off again downriver, rowing into the current just as it started to rain very heavily. Through the heavily falling rain it was difficult to see exactly where they were because it was advisable to stay in the fast flowing centre of the river lest they hit some overgrown outlying rocks that would previously be well above the waterline, on the bank.

It was late afternoon before the rain abated and they managed to see with astonishment how far they had come, for they knew from looking at the surrounding landscape that they were not far from the large falls, where the river plunged down the escarpment leaving the higher plains behind. Another few moments of travelling confirmed this as they could hear the water falling ahead of them. They hastily paddled into the nearest bank and secured the craft for the night. Buryl, Nem and Ingrit went forward to look at the falls and Ostric pleaded with them so that he could accompany his hero. At the edge of the falls they were amazed as they saw the river gushing down the middle of the escarpment and although they knew there were rocks and other pitfalls, they decided that in fact it would be worth trying to shoot down the rapids, particularly if the boat went first. Each raft with the full complement of twenty oarsmen might well make the passage in safety. So therefore, having checked that all the luggage was secure to the raft and that they too were well anchored, Thylux, Nem and Buryl re-boarded their boat and pushed out into the middle of the stream. With a mighty whoosh they were catapulted over the edge of the plain and then shot down the rapids at an astonishing speed. They found it best to row backwards which made their craft more manoeuvrable as it checked its own pace and was not going quite as quickly as the foaming river. Towards the end of the rapids there had been a twenty-foot almost vertical waterfall when they were going upriver, but now they could not stop their wild progress so they simply aimed where they thought the east river looked deepest and within moments had reached calmer waters at the bottom.

Although they had reached calmer waters their boat came down into the lake with such force that it almost went underwater, but it gradually shook itself clear of the undertow and bobbed up to the surface carrying the three men who had enjoyed the wild exciting water slide. They now steered for the bank of the swollen river and secured their boat to a firm stand of palm trees that was just on the waterline and they jumped ashore on to the damp sandy soil and began the long climb back up to the top where the four rafts waited. Although there were no signs of hostile robbers in the area they dared not leave the treasure unguarded, so Nem and Umlite with Ostric, who always liked to be with Nem, stood guard at the top of the river over the remaining three rafts whilst the other nineteen men took one of the rafts downriver in the same crazy whirlwind ride down the rapids.

They reached safety, but had to re-lash the treasure chests to the raft as some of the lashings had worn loose in the maelstrom ride. Then, leaving the raft under the guard of Buryl and two of the Watutsi tribesmen, the other sixteen under Thylux repeated the same journey again and again until by the end of the day the final craft was brought down the helter-skelter ride to the lake bottom just as the sun was setting. As they were all exhausted after the three days' enormous journey, they slept on the rafts under their makeshift tents which kept any rain off.

At dawn the following day, they continued their voyage north with the four rafts drifting along on the current following the small ship until by nightfall they came within sight of the city of Khartoum, where the two river Niles joined to become really fast-flowing as the main bulk of the water now seemed to be coming down the other stream to the east of the city. Here the city walls were still beside the river but the river was of course a lot higher and the barges together with the leading boat moored alongside the tavern that they had visited on their journey south. There were many excited Sudanese tradesmen who inquired after the treasures they brought but learning they had nothing to trade and that Thylux demanded to see the chieftain of the city once more, they sent an envoy to the palace and the chieftain came down himself to see them and congratulate them on the success of their quest.

With the pleasantries over, Thylux asked for news of Egypt and of what, if anything, was happening between Egypt and the growing Hittite empire.

The Sudanese chieftain said that, according to his messengers, the Pharaoh from the northern kingdom had marched north before the river started to flood in order to meet an invading army that was coming south, but he said, 'That is the last news that we have received and that is now many days old.'

Thylux thanked the king and politely refused the kind offer of staying for the night and said they must press forward as their army must know of the success of their quest.

Thylux then called for a council meeting between himself, Buryl, Nem, Ingrit and Umlite.

Thylux said, 'We have no time to lose – we must get back to our own country and make the treasure safe in the southern city of Luxor, under the guardianship of the southern king, and then we must speed northwards to join our army.'

Buryl said that they could continue on through Sudan, particularly as the other river which then joined them would take them faster than before, they should be safe travelling by night but would have to stop at the great cataract at Aswan where they entered Egypt. They agreed to split up and that the three soldiers from Egypt would sail on into the night to try to get to Luxor. Thylux told Ingrit and Umlite to follow on as quickly as they could but to go no further than the cataract at Aswan, where they hoped to have soldiers from the southern kingdom to meet them. Having agreed to this strategy, and although they were very tired, they decided to press on.

Unhitched from the four rafts, the sailing boat went streaming down the river far faster than a man running along the bank could keep up with, but even so it was not until the pearly grey light of morning which was lightening the sky to the east that they finally came to Aswan. After leaving their small boat moored at the top of the cataract they looked down and considered whether they dared a breakneck trip down the rapids in the boats. This time common sense prevailed and they decided not to rely on luck and not to tumble and gurgle over the wicked rocks. So they wearily up ended the boat and carried it down below to the bottom of the falls. By this time it was about midnight and they had not slept for thirty-six hours, but despite their fatigue, Thylux made them continue north-wards.

They shoved the boat away from the shore and once in the current they were gathering speed to their previous pace and Nem suddenly remembered that there was a group of islands when the water was lower and not in full flood.

He said to Thylux, 'We must be cautious when we shoot over those islands as we could easily rip the hull of the boat on some of the rocks that are normally well above the water level.'

Thylux agreed and tried to steer the boat towards the western shore to ensure that they kept well away from the islands. However the boat was in the grip of the current and would not respond to the tiller. Buryl shouted to Thylux that they must either travel slower than the current or faster, then that would give them steerage. As they were travelling so quickly and there was no moon to guide their path, they tried to slow the boat by rowing backwards which they did for a few minutes and gradually they managed to manoeuvre the boat towards the western bank. But they were all quite exhausted by the work and when they reached a calmer stretch of water, Thylux prudently anchored the boat and made it fast to the shore.

He said, 'We will sleep on the boat where we are for a couple of hours, just until we gain the strength to continue.'

Whilst they were beginning to curl themselves into comfortable sleeping positions Nem whispered to Thylux, 'I have some very important things that I must discuss with you, concerning the daughter of the southern kingdom.'

But Thylux had closed his eyes and was gently snoring. Nem glanced over at Buryl and saw that he too was asleep, so he sighed and quickly fell into a dreamless sleep, which was just as well because he did not see Thylux who opened his eyes again. He had not been sleeping but grinned hugely because he knew what Prince Nem wanted to ask him.

He murmured, 'Never mind, my prince, it will wait.'

Chapter Seventeen

Nem awoke when his shoulder was softly shaken by Thylux. He had only been asleep for a couple of hours and he wondered how on earth Thylux had woken up because he felt that he could easily go back to sleep for the rest of the day.

Thylux said gently, 'You need not wake Buryl, allow him to sleep a little longer. Now untie the boat and I will steer us into the main stream as the dawn is just beginning and we can see the way ahead.

'But before you move forward into the current you had better tell me the urgent thing that you mentioned before we slept.'

As Thylux stood up and went to the tiller, he pulled up the anchor and released the mooring lines to allow the boat to drift out into the current once more. Leaving the cold form of Buryl still asleep in the prow, Nem stood behind Thylux.

'The important matter that I wish to discuss,' said Nem, 'is that I need your advice on how to go about asking for Princess Vavia's hand in marriage.'

'Are you sure about this?' said Thylux. 'Marriage is a very serious undertaking particularly for a prince. You must remember that the woman you choose will be the queen of Egypt one day.' As he said these words Thylux tried to look very solemn.

Nem said, 'You are pulling my leg, you old rogue. Of course I have thought about all these things, and surely we can never tell if a person is suited to such a challenging task.' He continued swiftly, 'But we know that she is a princess and is of royal blood, so she should be well taught in the art of being a queen.'

'Yes, my prince, I am pulling your leg,' said Thylux, 'apart from which she is very beautiful,' he grinned. 'But I don't suppose you have thought about that,' he said with an even broader smile.

Nem was suddenly serious and said, 'Please do not tease me. I need your help as all these things are alien to me. How do I go about it?'

Thylux was quiet for a while and then said, 'Well to be honest, you should firstly seek your father's permission, but bear in mind the gravity of the situation, and the distinct possibility of battle with the Hittites, which will be a hard battle, as they are trained fighting men from the civilised world and not a bunch of wild native warriors like that Zulu posse. We will have a hard job, which is why we must reach the army with our good news as they will be shy of fighting if we withhold the knowledge of our success. So I think your father will allow your own judgement on this matter, which I think is very wise and a good choice.'

As Nem was still looking at him impatiently, he quickly continued, and said, 'You simply ask her, there really is no mystery to it.'

'But do I not have to offer a gift, like a dowry?' said Nem.

'Yes, my prince,' said Thylux, 'but do not forget we have four large barges upriver and they are full of treasure. I am sure your grandfather would not miss a small chest of selected items for his grandson's wedding, and one that would unite all of Egypt. I am sure your father would approve of your choice, and let me be honest with you, my prince, he has already said that that would be his wish. Apart from anything else, they could possibly reinforce our own army, for if we were defeated they would be next in line for the Hittite expansion.'

He added this diplomatic reasoning as a sound back-up to Nem, and then, as if considering the matter closed, he said, 'Now, see if we can get any more wind speed out of our boat, as we have now gone past the hidden rocks.'

Nem changed places as Thylux handed him the tiller then went forward. Nem was surprised that he did not wake Buryl, but instead sat in the middle of the boat. With an oar in each of his mighty hands, he rowed the small craft himself and they surged forwards even faster than the current. The huge man seemed tireless, and it was not long before in the early dawn they saw the outlines of the southern capital city of Luxor. Nem guided the boat right up to the bottom of the palace steps that were now sub-aquatic due to the swollen river, and Buryl awoke as they slid into the mooring. Thylux jumped out to secure the boat to the docking cleats.

He called back to Buryl, 'You stay here on guard whilst your prince and I see the king on urgent business.'

Leaving Buryl to tidy up the boat, Thylux and Nem sprinted up the steps in order to make the guards realise the urgency of their mission. When challenged at the top step Thylux demanded an audience with the king. They were ordered to wait in an antechamber, presumably whilst the king was awoken at this early hour and prepared to receive them. They were soon shown through into the palace main reception hall, to be greeted very warmly by the king.

'Why, Captain Thylux and Prince Nem, presumably on your way back from your quest, did you meet with success?'

Thylux responded, 'Yes indeed, Lord King, we have four barges laden with the treasure which are at this moment up river and they will need transportation around the great cataract at Aswan. Could we prevail on you to provide a force to meet them above the falls and help them transport the treasure down river?'

'But of course,' replied the king. 'I am so pleased that your quest met with success and am keen to learn the details from you,' he said expectantly.

'That, my lord king,' said Thylux, 'will have to wait, for I must know what news there is of our march against the Hittites.'

'Nothing more than that,' said the king, 'although I understand that there have been skirmishes toward the north, if not an actual battle, which I believe is imminent. All I know is that a message came from the Pharaoh that we were to muster reinforcements and be ready to send troops if needed, ready for battle.'

'This indeed is grim news,' said Thylux. 'I must journey north as my presence as captain of the royal guard will be urgently needed.'

'Mine as well!' chipped in Nem as if not to be left behind.

'Begging your pardon, my lord prince,' said Thylux, 'and although I am sure your absence from the army will be felt, I am sure the Pharaoh would prefer that you remain here south of the fighting, just in case things go ill for us, which I greatly fear might happen, without the news of our success,' said Thylux with a heavy heart.

Nem was about to argue but Thylux put a huge hand on his shoulder. 'On this matter, it is my command that you stay here, my prince, because that, I believe, is my Pharaoh's ardent wish.'

Thylux then turned to go but was stayed by the king.

'What I command is that you wait. You will be of little use in the exhausted state that you are now in,' the king said perceptively. 'You must stay for food and wine and a rest for that is my command.'

In reluctant agreement, Thylux sighed and said, 'So be it, but can you guard our boats and can you relieve my guard there? For they must continue north with me if Nem must remain here under your stewardship, lord king.'

Not wanting to miss out on a battle, Nem spoke out in objection.

'Your captain is right,' interjected the king, 'apart from which you can tell me the story of your quest and its great success, that must be recorded in the Great Book of Time.'

And so it was that food and wine were brought for the weary travellers, who were quickly joined by Buryl, and they ate their fill before retiring to rest.

They had slept for barely six hours when Thylux woke them and said, 'We have to continue our journey north-wards, so we must be ready to depart within the hour and sail along by night. I am afraid that you must stay here, Nem, as I know it would be your father's wish and he would be extremely annoyed with me if you came with me to do battle.'

'I understand,' said Nem, saluting his captain, 'but allow me this,' he said. 'I will have the rafts unloaded of their treasure where it will remain safe till returned to the Valley of Kings, where it belongs. Now each of the four rafts would be able to carry fifty fighting men from the reserve army that the king has been asked to muster. Now if I can ask the king to provide me with a force of two hundred that I could lead to help in your battle in the north, I am sure my father would agree to that.'

'Yes, my prince,' said Thylux, 'I am sure that we would greatly welcome such a force, but I can give you no such command and it will be up to the king if he allows it, but yes, I would be most grateful for such assistance.' He then turned to leave but had gone no further than a couple of paces when Nem called him back.

'And Thylux, it is my intention to speak to the princess tonight and ask her what we spoke of,' he said murmuring so that the others could not overhear the conversation. 'So with luck I will see you sooner than you think.'

'That indeed is wonderful news,' said Thylux, 'and please give my regards to Princess Vavia and I hope to see that all your plans come to bear fruit,' he said, and smiled indicating the double meaning to his words. And so he and Buryl left to sail north to join the army, and meet what fate had in store for them.

Chapter Eighteen

Nem walked around to the side of the palace that over-looked the river, and stood and watched Thylux and Buryl manoeuvre the boat into the red river. As he watched, a breeze from the south sprang up, and he saw Thylux unfurl the sail and the sailboat leapt forward under sail for the first time on its journey back home. Thylux looked back and saw Nem's golden wrist bracelets glint in the afternoon sun as he waved him goodbye. Thylux returned the wave and then turned his face northward as he and Buryl sailed onwards, leaving Nem still staring northward as their boat disappeared into the misty horizon.

Feeling that he was being watched, without turning around, Nem asked, 'How long have you been watching me?'

'Since you came to stand outside my balcony, Prince Nem,' said Vavia, 'and I truly delight in all that I see.'

Feeling his heart miss a beat, Nem turned around and bowed to the princess and said, 'I have very confused feelings, Princess Vavia. On the one hand I am being held against my wishes, under your father's stewardship, but I could hardly wish for a better keeper, which must include his household, for indeed I have been looking forward to seeing you again.'

The princess walked towards him and gazed with her beautiful, violet eyes and lovingly whispered, 'How I have prayed for your safe return, my lord.'

Nem reached out and put his arm around her shoulders and said, 'We return not only safely but with our quest mainly completed.'

And he told her of the four barges of treasure that would be waiting above the falls at Aswan. He then continued and said, 'I would like to offer your father some of the treasure in return for your hand in marriage.' He said this not realising that the words had rolled out so easily.

'Oh, Nem,' cried the princess, 'do you really mean it? For nothing would make me happier.'

'With your father's leave,' said Nem, as he held her in a warm embrace.

'That I will gladly accept,' said the king from the shadows, 'but do please step inside the palace as you are becoming a spectacle for the subjects in the city, and although you may make a handsome pair, I do not want my royal family to be the subject of idle gossip in the streets.'

It had all been so easy, thought Nem as he gazed down at his bride-to-be.

'The first treasure that I will take from my grandfather's hoard will be a ring of intent that shall be chosen by the princess herself,' said Nem.

As the princess seemed to be lost for words the king said, 'I thank you, my son, and will you prepare yourself to journey with my men to fetch these four barges of treasure that I am to store for the Pharaoh, until the bulk can be returned to its rightful place?'

'Yes indeed,' said Nem. 'When will you have your men ready?'

'They will be assembled within the hour,' said the king, 'one hundred of my finest troops who will be ready to march south as soon as you wish. As I understand, there are only twenty Watutsi men to guard the treasure and do not forget that there are many thieves and robbers in northern Sudan.'

The king then left the young couple, but as he left he called out, 'I will see you shortly, Prince Nem, when my guards will be ready to escort you up the river to Aswan.'

So after a brief farewell and promise to look after himself, Nem left his princess with her words ringing in his ears. As he entered the palace's entrance hallway he saw the king talking to a guard captain, a short but powerfully built man.

When the king saw him he called him over and said, 'Prince Nem, this is Captain Krater, who has one hundred men who are ready to march as soon as you wish. The captain is one of my finest guards and has fought many campaigns on our southern borders, so he knows the Sudanese, and all their tricks.' Captain Krater had a broad, honest face, with a quick smile and Nem took an instant liking to the man. As they descended the palace steps Nem asked if Captain Krater's men could run and not march as time was of very great importance, particularly bearing in mind what the king had said regarding the robbers, and of course Nem remembered the small skirmish that they had had with a robber band when they left on their journey south.

Captain Krater smiled and replied, 'They will do whatever I ask of them, Prince Nem, for we have been too long without action.'

And so it was that the heir to the throne of Egypt left the palace in the late afternoon with one hundred men, all trotting along the east bank of the swollen river. The men were all fresh and so kept up the fast pace until well after nightfall, when they reached the Island of the Elephant and it was then that Nem realised why it had such a name, as it looked like an elephant standing in the river, with the water covering its legs. He had seen such elephants on his long journey south. They halted for a short while, whilst the men broke the rations they had brought with them and revived themselves with drinks of clear water, that they additionally carried with them.

Whilst the men were tidying up, Nem, who was still quite tired, but didn't want to admit it, said to Captain Krater, 'It is easier to climb the falls on this side of the river, because on our journey south we found a good part on other bank.'

Captain Krater now said, 'That part will now be underwater, as that is part of the falls when the river is in full flow. But there is a good trek on this bank which is still above the level of the river.'

They then trotted on for another two hours until they reached the bottom of the falls.

'We will rest here,' said Captain Krater, 'as there is no point in climbing upriver until it is light.'

So, they all gratefully made camp, after Captain Krater had set the guard, which would change every two hours.

Nem was awoken at first light and sat for a few moments with churning thoughts until his mind called him back to reality and he had to ask Captain Krater what he had just said. Captain Krater realised how tired Prince Nem was as he repeated his earlier question.

'Do you want the men to have breakfast here or to climb up the falls first?'

'I think we should press on,' said Nem, 'as we can always eat at the top, if everything is okay with the barges.'

So, quickly re-packing, they began the climb up beside the raging torrent, which took quite a long time as the main path was lower down the hillside and at this time of year was well below the flood line of the great river. They eventually reached the top level, where the comparatively still waters began their maddening cascade down the steep rocky face of the borderland between northern Sudan and southern Egypt.

Nem and Captain Krater looked around but could see no treasure-laden rafts until one of the scouts pointed towards the western bank. In the haze, created by the silvery mists arising from the waterfall, they could see the four great rafts secured to a group of trees whose roots were still well below the water level of the flooded river. They were beyond hailing distance of the rafts which they could only just make out and then, in the haze, they realised that the rafts were being kept offshore by the Watutsi tribesman, who were keeping them from drifting ashore by constantly battling with the river bank. Surprised by this, Nem and Captain Krater climbed higher up the rocks to their left in order to try and see what was stopping the Watutsi tribesman from running the rafts ashore. They climbed to a high ledge and when they again looked out to the west they saw the reason why the Watutsis were battling furiously to ensure that the rafts were kept away from the shore. There was a large gathering of Sudanese bandits on the western shore who were waiting for the rafts to come within boarding range. Cursing their misfortune at coming up the eastern bank they wondered how they could get across the water to the Watutsis and be of assistance, because it was fairly evident that the current was too strong to paddle the rafts back to the eastern shoreline and if the Watutsis released the lines mooring the rafts to the trees they would be swept over the falls to their certain death. Realising that urgent action was needed, Nem asked Captain Krater if he or any of his men would be able to swim across the river.

The captain sadly shook his head and said, 'Apart from the great distance, the current is too strong in the middle of the river for me or any of my men, as I would not ask them to do what I could not do myself.'

Carefully considering these words, Nem, who was taller than any of the southern guards and very broad across the shoulders, felt that he would have to swim the distance

himself, as he was a strong and powerful swimmer. Asking
how much rope they had brought with them he started
walking quickly up river to a point some distance away
where the rocks jutted a long way into the flooded waters.
Learning that they had brought a lot of rope with them he
slipped off his helmet, leather breastplate and his golden
bracelets, which he passed to Captain Krater with the
instruction that they be guarded, and requested that a
length of the rope be tied about his waist.

Wading out from the end of the rocks Nem shortly
reached waist height in the flooded river. He called back to
Captain Krater to haul him back if it looked as though he
would be washed over the waterfall, and added that if and
when he reached the nearest raft, they were to attach a
thicker rope to the line so that it could be pulled over to the
raft which could then be towed back to the eastern shoreline. Nem then plunged into the water and, greatly
refreshed by the cool water, struck out strongly across the
river. Although he realised that he was swimming as
powerfully as he could he was getting washed down stream
by the current. He therefore altered his aim to a point
further down the bank than the rafts and struck out again
for the far side of the river. It seemed as if he had been
swimming for ages and he realised that his strength was
fading fast when he heard a splashing noise behind him and
glanced back to see that two male crocodiles were fighting
in the river. Realising that he was doomed if he relaxed his
pace he swam harder than ever for the eastern bank and
soon realised that he was being pursued by the crocodiles.
Swimming as fast as he could, he suddenly began to hear
shouts from the Watutsi on the nearest raft to him, encour-
aging him to reach his goal. He had used the last of his
strength and was thinking that it was a strange way to
complete the quest that was so close to success and on the
day after he had become engaged to marry the beautiful

Princess Vavia, when strong arms pulled him on to the bamboo floor of the raft. He turned and looked up to see Ingrit smiling down at him.

He gasped and said, 'Untie the rope from around my waist and haul it aboard the raft,' which they did and soon found that it was attached to a far stronger line that would haul the raft back across to the eastern bank.

The rope was swiftly secured to the raft and making sure the rafts were still secured in line, one to the other, with shorter stretches of tough rope, he ordered all twenty Watutsi men to get back on to Ingrit's raft and paddle as well as being hauled back by the team of one hundred soldiers, led by Captain Krater. Much to the despairing cries of the Sudanese bandits, the line of rafts was soon heading towards the eastern bank. Even though they paddled very hard and were being pulled at the same time, the fourth raft was being towed toward the falls by the strong current. However, Captain Krater had seen this possibility and suddenly the towing line was pulled a lot harder towards the eastern bank because the towing party were marching backwards with the line to ensure the safety of all four rafts.

Captain Krater was astonished at how ingeniously constructed the rafts were and how quickly they were dismantled and made portable. Returning Nem's golden bracelets, Captain Krater insisted on carrying Nem's helmet and sturdy leather breastplate.

'It is no trouble for me to carry these, Prince Nem, as you must be tired from your arduous race against the current and the pursuing crocodiles.'

With all one hundred soldiers transporting the treasure and the rafts that had been dismantled into their three main sections – the two heavy, wooden pontoons and the rolled up bamboo floor section of the rafts – they fairly soon had everything moved down to the base of the falls.

Chapter Nineteen

Having brought everything down the rock face, the rafts were quickly reassembled and then refloated in the river. The treasure and the dead Pharaoh's sarcophagus were then relashed on to the bamboo flooring. Captain Krater said to Prince Nem that he could travel back downriver with the rafts, allowing his men to return on foot. But Prince Nem said that there was surely room for all the men if they were divided equally, twenty-five to a raft. Prince Nem said this so that he could see whether the rafts really would hold two hundred men, as he had suggested to Thylux. The added weight of twenty-five men per raft did not seem to make them much lower in the water, although they were more sluggish, but that could be compensated by more men paddling with makeshift implements used as paddles. Then, resecuring the four rafts in line, they pushed away from the shore and the sluggish rafts moved slowly out into the current and were then racing along almost as fast as a man could run. All the soldiers were grateful for the rest as it had been a hard forced march up to Aswan and the episode of towing the rafts back across to the east bank, unloading the treasure and bringing everything down the steep face beside the falls, had been hard work indeed.

Prince Nem on the first raft talked to Captain Krater about how many men were in the army in the south and whether or not they would be willing to join the northern army as reinforcements. Captain Krater told Nem that they had at least five hundred troops and by mustering every man capable of fighting they could muster another three hundred. The captain also said that they would be more than happy to be involved in a full battle rather than just guarding the border against invading bandit tribes from the Sudan. Nem, who had great respect for Captain Krater, then asked him if he would be willing to come with his two hundred men as immediate reinforcements, provided that the king would grant that wish. Captain Krater said that they would be more than willing to go, and added that if they stressed to the king the urgency of this situation, being that if the northern army were defeated, the Hittites would then have plenty of time to build a far larger force that could capture all of Egypt, whilst sending reinforcements at this early stage would help great Egypt to smash the invading force. So the plan was settled.

They reached Luxor by mid-evening and found the palace in a ready state to meet them. They took the treasure to a locked, large storeroom where it would lay until it was safe to return it the Valley of the Kings. Prince Nem was keen to see Princess Vavia who greeted him with a warm embrace and said that she wanted to know all the details of their adventure. Prince Nem told her the rough details of their exploits, making little of his own part in rescuing the rafts from the western river bank, and she gazed up at him in love and wonder at his calmness when in danger.

But he then held the princess in a tight embrace and he said, 'I am truly sorry, my darling, but I will have to ask your father to release me to go north with the reinforcements in the battle against the invading Hittites.'

There were tears in her eyes when she looked up at him and said, 'It would be wrong of me to try and stop you because I know that you must do this thing, but I will pray ardently for your safe return and make plans for us to be married.'

And so it was that Prince Nem went with Captain Krater to petition him to allow him to continue north on the rafts with two hundred men under Captain Krater's command. The king considered the request and agreed that it might just ensure victory against the Hittites, but said he was unsure of whether he should allow Prince Nem to go north. But Nem said that he alone knew the river well enough and that he had previously discussed this plan with Thylux who would intercede with Pharaoh on his behalf, which persuaded the king that it would be in his best interests to let prince Nem go with the reinforcements.

But he said, 'You are to be very careful, my son, as it would break my daughter's heart if anything happened to you and I indeed would also be sad to lose a good prospective son-in-law, a man who could completely unite Egypt into a truly great power.'

The king continued, 'But tonight you feast here, stay the night and leave first thing in the morning as the troops will not be totally ready before then.'

And so it was agreed that they spent their last night in the luxury of the palace of Luxor before sailing north at dawn the following morning.

The following day dawned bright and clear, and as Nem stepped aboard the leading raft he was pleased to see that each raft had now been fitted with double triangular sails, one on the left front and one on the right back. These would help to steer the raft as well as give it extra speed if there was a following wind, which there normally was at this time of year. Even fifty men on the raft dressed in their full war gear did not weigh down the rafts as heavily as all the treasure had done and as they pushed away from the quayside the small triangular sail billowed out with the following breeze that blew from the south. With ten of the soldiers on each side of the raft, dipping in long paddles, they quickly pulled into the main stream of the river and paddled into the north. Nem glanced back to the palace where Princess Vavia stood next to the king and waved him away with the sunlight glittering off the ring that she had selected from the treasure. It was in pale gold and was set with lapis lazuli of the deepest blue, which complemented the main stone which was a large deep red garnet. And Nem felt sure that his grandfather would have approved of what the ring was now depicting, his intended betrothal and the joining of the two kingdoms, something which Nem's grandfather and father had attempted but never fully succeeded in establishing. The other gifts, mainly of silver and gold, were but a mere handful of the old Pharaoh's treasure, and Nem had an accurate list to show to his father of his full bridal dowry that had been taken from the treasure chest of the long-dead Pharaoh.

The journey back downriver took even less time as they were moving downriver with the current and under sail with ten men outside each raft paddling. And as there were plenty of spare willing hands, the paddlers changed whenever they needed a rest. Nem sat looking at the countryside that was now flooded and covered with new soil that the great river had brought down with its annual flood, and he knew that this meant that there would be an excellent harvest that year, as the seed would be sown into the damp earth as soon as the water receded and the new earth that the river brought down always brought a good harvest as it was very rich in nutrients. The water was beginning to drain away from the flooded fields and the hot sun which shone brightly over the damp earth would quickly dry up the excess water. Nem was wondering how he could retain some of the water for use at another date when his thoughts were turned back to the present time by Captain Krater, who asked him, 'What's the normal battle position the army uses?'

Nem said it depended on the generals and the layout of the land which was chosen to do battle, but said that the normal strategy was that a long shield wall would be formed by the front ranks that would engage the enemy front line. Such shield wall battles then became more of a pushing match but then their shield wall would deliberately break in a couple of places to allow a spear thrust of attacking swordsmen through into the enemy ranks.

Captain Krater replied that that had been used so often that it would be wiser to employ a new tactic.

Nem was enthralled by Captain Krater's honesty and asked whether they used a change of tactics in the south. Nem listened very carefully to all of Captain Krater's ideas and then thought of how some of his own army captains, like Thylux, would make good generals but often were not even given a chance to try out new ideas. He gradually deduced that a lot of the ancient generals had perhaps been in place for too long and it was now time for a change. As his thoughts wandered through battle strategy, and the way that troops should be led, he realised that the day was wearing on and that they were approaching the Sphinx, which guarded the entrance to the Valley of the Kings.

The rafts were racing along the river, the men rowing two abreast, and as they continued into the night he told Ingrit, who had never been this far north before, that they would continue into the night, as they would reach his home palace before too long, and then find out what news there was from their army, and where it was stationed.

There was no moon that night, but the stars were very bright and seemed to glow with the intensity of godly light to force him to believe that the gods were trying to tell him something, and he thought back to when Chithra had taught him many years ago. As he thought of Chithra, his old teacher, he suddenly remembered about the Greek fire that could be used very effectively by the enemy, and of how Chithra longed to know the secret of how to make it.

He suddenly realised that the palace was now in sight and that they were being hailed from its quayside and so, by altering the position of the sails, they guided the rafts into the bank and moored their rafts at the steps to the palace and Nem led Ingrit and Captain Krater back into his old home.

Realising that the waiting reception at the door of the palace was hosted by Chithra himself, he bounded up the last few steps and greeted his old teacher with a great hug that lifted Mithras off his feet.

'How you have grown in the few months since I last saw you,' said Chithra as he regained his feet, 'and how well you look – or will look when you have washed away the grime from your journey!' He quickly continued, and said that Thylux and Buryl had returned home a few days ago with the excellent news of their quest and that he could bring them up to date with his news over dinner, which would be ready as soon as they had washed. Thylux and Buryl were back with the army that was a full day's march to the north-east where they would go tomorrow.

He clapped Nem on the back as lots of questions seemed to tumble out from Nem and laughingly said, 'Hush your noise, young Nem, all your questions can wait until you have cleaned yourself up and introduced us to your companions and then eat and discuss what we must now do, for there is much that is waiting to be done!'

After they had all washed and showered, and much to Ingrit's amazement, re-oiled their bodies, which seemed to make them glow as well as giving them a more fragrant scent, they went through into the main dining hall of the palace, where a grandiose feast was laid out. Again, this amazed Ingrit, as he thought that as the country was at war, they would have to live more frugally than this, but then realised how great and wealthy this country really was.

They sat down to the meal and Nem introduced Captain Krater, who was sitting on his left and said, 'Here on my right is a man who has become a very close friend, and has been a great help in the success of our quest,' and so saying introduced Ingrit to Chithra and the other palace officials. Nem went on to explain about his betrothal to Princess Vavia and his retrieval of the rafts. 'The treasure is now safely stored in the king's palace at Luxor.'

He then went on to tell them about the reinforcements that he had brought under Captain Krater and asked Chithra why he was not with Pharaoh and the army. Chithra answered with a full explanation that when they had originally sailed up the coast, they had been attacked by the Phoenicians, who, as he had predicted, used Greek fire against their highly inflammable reed galleys and that the army had only just escaped by putting to shore. They had lost two of the army's main generals, but they were now safely encamped on the borders of the Sinai desert and that he had come back to the palace with a sample of the Greek fire to try to discover its secret of combustibility.

Chapter Twenty

After supper, when everyone returned to their beds, Chithra took Nem by the arm and asked him to follow him. Chithra led Nem into his own quarters and to his work bench in his study where various potions were stored in jars.

Chithra said to Nem, 'I do not want you to tell anyone about this yet, but I have discovered the secret of making Greek fire. But it is a very volatile liquid that has to be made just before it can be used. It needs to be put in a sealed globe with a fuse attached, which is then lit, and the globe should then be catapulted at the object. Now whilst you were bathing before dinner, I slipped out to have a close look at the rafts that you came downriver on, as Buryl had told me about their construction. Now I believe that these would make ideal platforms on which we could build a very efficient catapult, and we could then use the Greek fire to its greatest advantage.'

Whilst he was saying this, he grabbed charcoal and a sheet of papyrus and sketched what he had in mind. He told Nem that what he would like to do would require Nem's agreement and authority, as being the Pharaoh's son his instructions would not be questioned by anyone.

'By now Thylux should have been promoted, because that was Pharaoh's intention when I came back to study the sample of Greek fire that I had obtained. He spoke to me of his plan to promote Thylux into one of the dead general's positions, so this is what I propose. I would like you to write a note to General Thylux, on a sealed scroll carried by your friend Captain Krater, ostensibly as a letter of introduction, at least that is what I would like you to tell Captain Krater. However, it would really be a letter telling Thylux that we will come along the coast in the rafts which can then hurl the globes of Greek fire at the Hittite army, but we will need to know the spot at which Thylux would like us to aim, so tell him to send an acknowledgement of the receipt of the letter with the plan of where we should attack the Hittite army. This, along with the reinforcements that you have brought, could well make the difference that we need to defeat the Hittites and Phoenicians. I am telling you this because I believe that we may have an informer in our midst, which is not surprising as we have a lot of the old Hittite troops in our army. I want no one but yourself and Thylux to know this. We will then send Captain Krater with a guide to take him to the Egyptian army whilst we make alterations to the rafts and install the catapults and quantities of Greek fire. We then require a small team to operate the catapults and help sail the rafts along the coast.'

At this point Nem interrupted Chithra and said that the ideal people to alter the rafts and man them would, if he could gain their agreement, be the Watutsis.

Chithra asked excitedly, 'Do you think they would do this?'

Nem said, 'I think that Ingrit would love the chance to fight for us.' They spent the next hour making plans and writing the letters on papyrus that were then rolled into scrolls and sealed with wax seals emblazoned with Nem's sign, which was embossed on one of his rings. It was early morning by the time they had finished, and then they went to bed for a few hours' sleep before they were roused again at the break of day.

Over breakfast, which Ingrit considered to be a veritable feast as there were fillets of fish, drumsticks of chicken, dates, pomegranates, oranges, peaches and other fruits that he did not recognise as well as wheat cakes, lotus bread, corn yoghurt and lots of other dishes, all placed on silver trays on a table from which they helped themselves, Nem told Ingrit and Captain Krater that he would send the Captain on in advance and provide a guide to take them to the army where he was due to report to Thylux, who Captain Krater was surprised and delighted to hear was now a general. As soon as they had finished breakfast he went down with Captain Krater to the assembled troops and gave him the appropriate sealed scrolls to give to General Thylux.

He introduced Captain Krater to the guide who would direct them to the army and said, 'The general will send me a reply by one of his messengers, but he will direct you into the appropriate battle stations.'

He added, 'I am sure General Thylux would be interested to hear some of your battle strategies that we discussed on the journey north.'

And with those words ringing in the captain's ears he waved them away.

He then turned to Ingrit and said, 'This will not mean goodbye, my friend,' as he put his arm around Ingrit's shoulder on the way back up the steps into the palace. He then continued and said, 'I have a special request of you, but please do not feel that you have to agree to the request because I will not think any the worse of you if you refuse.'

Ingrit, who was initially not marching with Captain Krater, said to Nem, 'If I can be of any service I would particularly like to fight for your army, as would all my small band of Watutsi warriors, so if that is your question the answer is undoubtedly yes.'

Nem laughed and said, 'I thought and hoped you would say that, but what I think I first want you to do is to help us to make some alterations to the rafts and then use them to go into battle against the Hittites and Phoenicians. It will be a hard and difficult and certainly very dangerous task, and I would not ask it of any lesser man.'

'You already have my answer,' said Ingrit. 'We would be delighted, just show us what you would like us to do.'

So Nem led Ingrit down to the rafts where Chithra was already waiting with a team of carpenters and masons. Nem called on Chithra and informed him that his guess of Ingrit hoping to join in battle was indeed correct, and that his Watutsi warriors were good sailors very keen to learn of his plans and would help with the conversion work.

Nem stood and watched as two catapults were erected roughly in the middle of each raft, each catapult being enormous, pivoted near one end on which a counter-balance of large stones was carried in a mesh net. When the net was full of heavy stones, it would pull the pivoted catapult into a vertical position. At the other end of the raft a wickerwork bowl was fitted to the arm. This was obviously to hold the globe of Greek fire that would send it flying through the air when the arm was winched back to below the vertical position. The throwing range and height could be altered by the weight of stones placed in the net, by the restraining force and by moving the restraining bar which checked the throwing arm of the catapult.

This work took most of the day and when Nem and Chithra were satisfied with the testing of the catapults, Chithra sent a message up to his work bench where he had put the mixture that made the Greek fire. He had some brought down to the rafts, then, with the expert Watutsi warriors waiting and eagerly watching, he and Nem filled a globe, made of hardened clay especially for the job, with the two mixtures. They then sealed the globe with a twist of rag that was soaked in oil, the globe was placed in the wicker basket of the prepared catapult, and the raft was manoeuvred to throw the globe across the wide river at the supposed target. Much to the Watutsis' amazement the rag on the globe was then lit, the shackle pin holding the winched arm was knocked out by Nem, and the catapult arm whistled through ninety degrees until it was checked by the restraining bar. This threw the globe well across the wide river to land on the target area where it immediately burst and exploded into masses of burning liquid. The Watutsis were absolutely amazed by this contraption and quite overjoyed when Mithras informed them that they would be the ones who would use this new weapon against the enemies of great Egypt.

It was then about late afternoon. He said that they had the rest of the day to practise throwing rocks of the appropriate weight and size as the globes because they did not have a great deal of globes and Greek fire to use on experimental firing. Nem joined Chithra and told the excited Watutsis that they hoped to sail after dinner so that they would not be seen from land. The excited Watutsi warriors quickly got the hang of using the catapults and were very eager to depart that evening after dinner. Leaving the Watutsis to continue their practice, Nem and Chithra returned to the palace to clean up before their final dinner, change into their war gear and bring down maps of where they were going. They then had dinner sent down to the Watutsis whom they joined and then prepared to sail due north-west.

Shortly after darkness had fallen, with everything stowed neatly on board – additional rock weights, hundreds of newly baked, empty clay globes and urns of the two ingredients that made the Greek fire – they sailed down-river until they met the sea. This again was a brand new experience for the Watutsis, who thought at first it was a large lake until they tasted the water and realised that it was not freshwater but saltwater and the smell of the ozone and the slight iodine flavour of the air had an amazingly invigorating effect upon them all. Keeping within sight of land, they sailed north-west along the coastline until they spotted a bright signal fire on the headland. It was then a few hours before sunrise and they anchored the rafts in a shallow bay, ready for the morning light.

They briefly rested, but ensured that a close watch was kept and that no light was seen on the rafts which could give away their presence to foreign eyes. When dawn eventually came, a small boat was rowed out from the headland just to their north east, and much to Mithras and Nem's pleasure and excitement it contained an Egyptian army messenger, who came on board and bowed before Prince Nem and handed him a letter from General Thylux. Hastily opening the letter, Nem and Chithra spread open a chart of the area and noted on it their position and marked on it the position of the Egyptian troops, who were just further to the north around the headland. Facing them was the Hittite army, which was being fed from the sea by the Phoenician galleys, which were constantly bringing food and reinforcements. There was a small harbour and a makeshift quayside where the Phoenician galleys were unloading men and food. This area was marked as the target for them to attack when a new signal fire was lit on the headland. Their orders were fairly clear; Thylux wanted them to hinder and harass the unloading of new troops which would draw men away from the Hittite army when he planned to attack. They set sail north to just before the headland to await the signal.

Chapter Twenty-One

General Thylux was in council with all his captains. First he introduced Captain Krater from the southern army and he said, 'They will stand in reserve, and then be used as a counter-attack when our centre line makes a mock retreat.'

This was an entirely new strategy to the assembled captains and some of them spoke up in protest.

He calmed them by saying, 'Now most of you know that our quest was successful and I can now tell you that the body of the dead Pharaoh, and the stolen treasure is safely locked in the palace at Luxor, in the southern kingdom. But I must ask you to keep quiet about this so that our enemies might believe that we are dispirited.'

He then told them that the strategy that they would use would be to send out flanking forces primarily of archers, and then the central force would attack. When it met with fierce resistance, as was expected, it would retreat, drawing in a pursuing counter-attack. However, at the same time, the outflanking arms would advance, and when the counter-offence came, the archers would rain down arrows on the attacking shield wall, as their heads and backs would be exposed. He continued by telling them that at this point their counter-attack would flounder and then the southern troops standing in reserve would attack behind a shield wall that the retreating central force would attach themselves to. At that point the outflanking forces would form a shield wall which would then move in to crush the Hittite army. This was, of course, an adaptation of the Zulu strategy, and he hoped that being a total new format that the Egyptians had never used before, it was to be a manoeuvre that would totally confuse their opponents. Even then he spoke nothing of the Greek fire catapults and, when questioned about the Phoenician galleys, he simply said that they should not have to worry about them.

The assembled captains considered this was a good and rational idea and went on to discuss further details of which sections would take on which role, and it was decided that the outflanking soldiers would be accompanied by a shield wall to protect their backs, but then would move in front of them, for the final crushing blow to the Hittite army. Thylux sent a further message to Nem on the rafts that if the bombardment of the galleys was successful, he could then turn his Greek fire on to the central mass of the Hittite army.

The captains left the briefing session to ready their troops to attack at dawn and at the same time a small party went to the headland to light a signal fire. Just before dawn a messenger rowed out to Prince Nem on the rafts with Thylux's detailed plans. Chithra and Nem were very excited by Thylux's plan, so just before dawn they quietly paddled the rafts around the headland, where they could see the makeshift quayside where the Phoenician galleys were coming to dock.

Right on time, the signal fire came to light and at the same time the already prepared catapults released eight Greek fire globes at the docking galleys. These fire globes slightly overshot their target and smashed on the quayside, which had a great effect as the quayside burst into bright flame and silhouetted the galleys against the burning quayside, where panicking troops were diving into the sea to escape the fire. At the same time the Hittite army was distracted by the fire that was at their backs and many of their forces turned in confusion to watch the spectacle unfolding. At this point the central force of the Egyptian army attacked the Hittite shield wall which was in some confusion and their first thrust penetrated deep into the Hittite army where many fierce individual battles were fought and hand-to-hand fighting was extremely fierce.

Then the second salvo of Greek fire bombs was discharged; the Watutsis had corrected the range of the missiles, and they rained down on the docking galleys with deadly effect. The galley captains realised what was happening, but could not see where the attack was coming from because the catapult rafts were out at sea to their west and still in the darkness as the sun rose in the east. Also, the fire from the burning quayside blinded their night vision. The galleys could neither dock nor go back to sea, as all the men on board were fighting the fires as more and more fire bombs rained down on them. The Hittite army was still in a confused state and the fierce fighting escalated, until the Hittites, rallying around their standard bearer, began a concerted effort to push back the Egyptian force, which they outnumbered by two to one. The Hittite general ordered his captains to abandon the Phoenician galleys and concentrate on their battle against the Egyptian army. The Egyptian assault was then met with fierce resistance but had already inflicted a savage blow to the Hittites.

As the Hittites rallied, the order came from Thylux to start the mock retreat, which did have the desired effect of drawing the counter-attack after it, and a new shield wall was formed by the Hittites who charged in strong formation after the retreating Egyptians. At that point the outflanking arms of the Egyptian army which had been advancing on either side were quite unnoticed by the Hittites because their attention was either on the fight or the inferno behind them. The Egyptian archers fired scores of piercing arrows on to the Hittite army, and in particular at the exposed backs of their shield wall. Once again there was confusion in the Hittite ranks and their counter-attack was quickly neutered whilst their captains tried desperately to rally their troops. Then the retreating Egyptians suddenly turned and were swallowed into an advancing shield wall that hit the Hittite army with resounding impact and was a solid phalanx of tightly held shields from the southern army, led by Captain Krater.

The Phoenician galleys were blackened, burning hulks, as they had been abandoned by the Hittites and their captains were desperately trying to douse the fire and then row back away, with no intention of helping the Hittite army that was beginning to buckle under the pressure from the new Egyptian attack. Seeing the destruction that they had wreaked on the Phoenician galleys, Nem and Chithra redirected their remaining firebombs into the backs of the Hittite army, with devastating force. The Hittites were brave fighters but they were being totally crushed as they had been completely outmanoeuvred and as the fighting continued and the piles of dead mounted, the carnage flourished and still more firebombs showered down on the Hittite, who then started to surrender.

The battle lasted only twenty minutes from beginning to end but there were still pockets of resistance amongst the Hittites who had fought to the last man whilst the victorious Egyptian army was taking captive prisoners from the remaining Hittite resistance.

But, unnoticed by Thylux, a rogue force of the Hittite fighters completely outflanked the Egyptians and were attacking Pharaoh's encampment which was placed behind the Egyptian army. However, this action was noticed by Nem and the Watutsis who had fired the last of their Greek firebombs. On Nem's orders they paddled hard for the shore. Prince Nem leapt into the foaming breaking waves as the raft struck dry ground and drawing his sword led a host of screaming Watutsi spearmen into the Hittite force.

The invading Hittite force of about fifty men were attacking Pharaoh, who was defended by Thylux and four of the royal guard, but they were well outnumbered. Thylux thought how ironic it was that he would probably die on the day his army had won a resounding victory when his spirits were renewed as he saw Prince Nem, leading twenty Watutsi spearmen, come charging up the beach. Although there were fifty in the tight force they did not expect the violent attack that they encountered from this tall golden figure, whose sword flashed like a ray of sun in the morning light as he chopped down two attackers, and they were terrified by the tall black Watutsi spearmen each of whom looked like the devil himself. They very quickly yielded and dropped their weapons and sank to their knees begging for mercy.

Pharaoh stood tall and commanding, he raised his hands and shouted in a deep booming voice, 'Halt, we will not mar our victorious day with the needless slaughter of cowardly troops.'

He turned to Nem and simply said, 'Welcome home, my son, it is good to see you.'

Although the battle was over, it took the rest of the day to form some order out of the chaos and carnage. There were comparatively few Hittites who surrendered and the death toll was staggeringly high. The alliance between the Phoenicians and the Hittites had been completely severed, so no Hittites were ferried back home. They had been completely vanquished.

In the next few days after the battle, when the dead were buried with the necessary honour and the injured were sent to the houses of healing, Prince Nem spent a lot of his time with Chithra, telling him of his ideas for reform of the army and the idea of storing a lot of the flood water that drained away, by the use of large underground silos or water chambers that could be cut from the living rock and then recovered with topsoil, so that the only entry to obtain the water would be from a well. This would solve the problem of evaporation and wasted drainage and then water would be on hand as and when needed in the hot summer sunshine.

On the third day after the battle, Pharaoh summoned Nem to his tent.

'My son, I have heard a lot of wonderful stories about the success of your quest, and how you contributed to that success. I have also learnt with great interest about your betrothal to Princess Vavia, which indeed meets with my wholehearted approval.'

He then arose from his throne and walked over to his son and put his arm around his shoulder and shooed away the few guards who were within hearing distance. He stared into his son's eyes and Nem gazed back and realised that his father was getting quite an elderly man as there were deep wrinkles around his eyes and his hair was turning white.

Pharaoh continued and said, 'Nem, my son, I am not long for this world, for my doctors tell me that I am dying and day by day I am growing weaker.' Alarm filled Nem's face, but his father calmed him with a raised finger and said, 'Fret not, my son, my death is not that imminent, and I hope to live some years yet.'

A long silence followed as father and son gazed into each other's eyes.

Pharaoh then said, 'But that is enough talk of what must happen and now we must make plans for your wedding and the final uniting of our great country. For indeed I want this thing to happen very soon and hopefully I can see my grandchildren before I leave this world for the next. Then you will become the god-king, and a very great Pharaoh you will make, as you are already thinking about your plans for the kingdom when it is yours to rule.'

'Tomorrow we will begin the journey back to our palace, but I have already sent a royal guard to bring Princess Vavia and her father and his guard to come for your wedding feast.' Pharaoh half turned to face the doorway as two men entered.

'Behold,' he said, 'the great lion of Egypt, General Thylux and the new captain of your royal household guards, Captain Buryl.' Prince Nem's face shone with pleasure as the three friends were united once again and there was great happiness and wonderful pleasure in knowing that they all shared a great future.